NANA

C.L. SUTTON

CHAPTER ONE

I glance at Peter and grin at his charming, sweet face. He always complains that his nose is too big; I like to call it *manly*. Then, he claims he looks *old,* whereas I like to use *distinguished*. He pushes his almost-black hair out of his eyes and squints at the dark road in front of us, blurred by the torrential rain. His eyebrows are practically meeting in the middle, and I stifle a giggle so as not to interrupt his concentration.

I touch his thigh and give the firm muscle a little squeeze. It feels good and excitement bubbles in my stomach. Peter drops his hand from the steering wheel and pats the top of mine. I grin at his wedding band sparkling up at me. I'm still trying to get used to that. He quickly returns his hand to the wheel. He's too cautious to risk navigating these tight bends one-handed. I like that about him.

Lightning slashes through the darkness, its jagged claws sinking into the foreboding countryside that surrounds us.

A shiver creeps up my spine, followed by a colossal yawn. Every muscle in my body aches from lugging boxes around all day and I eagerly anticipate sinking into my new, luxurious king-size bed that was dropped off by the delivery guys earlier today.

'Are we nearly there yet?' I ask Peter, aware of how childish I sound.

He smiles, warming every feature on his handsome face. 'Almost, honey. Only a few minutes to go.'

Despite our new house being only thirty miles from my old apartment, the weather has slowed us down and the twists and turns of the country lane are treacherous, forcing Peter to drive at less than half the speed limit. Driving out of the city into such desolation feels like we've journeyed to another planet.

'It's quiet out here,' I whisper into the darkness. I'm used to the hustle and bustle of Birmingham city centre. I don't think I'll be kept awake out here by drunken fights and the sounds of sirens.

Peter pats my hand again. 'You'll love it, Jen. I promise. Thistlewood is beautiful. Small, but it has everything we'll need. A couple of shops, a pub, even a little community centre.' He's told me all of this already, of course, but I love it when he talks about our future.

'Tell me about the house.'

'I don't have to. You'll see it for yourself soon.'

'Please, Peter. I'm excited.' And I want to distract myself from the terrifying drive.

He chuckles. 'It's nothing spectacular, but it has great potential. I know you'll wave your magic wand and it'll become our little palace. Three bedrooms, semi-detached, quiet cul-de-sac. You'll love it.'

I know I will. It's a far cry from the one-bedroom apartment I share with Mum. *Shared* with Mum.

I push away my grief. I'm not going to let anything ruin tonight.

Thunder bellows, making me duck.

Peter laughs at me. 'Oh, honey. Are you scared of thunder?'

'No, it just made me jump.' He laughs again, mocking the fear in my voice. He throws me a glance and opens his mouth wide, his signal for another gummy bear. I take one out of the bag and hold it up to check the colour. Green – his favourite. I go to pop it into his mouth.

'Shiiiit!' Peter suddenly screams, drawing out the curse word until the car screeches to a stop. My neck snaps forward and my forehead slams into the dashboard as the tyres finally catch the wet surface of the road.

We sit in silence, our panting breaths clouding the windscreen. Peter's gummy bears lie scattered across the dashboard, catching the moonlight like little colourful gems.

What happened?

Peter has turned a nasty shade of white. I touch his shoulder, but he doesn't acknowledge me.

'Did I hit her?'

'Who?'

He stares out the front window in shock, not answering me. The rain continues to thunder down, hammering the car angrily, briefly muted every couple of seconds by the swishing rhythm of windscreen wipers.

I squint into the headlight beams cutting through the black outside. There's no one there.

Peter slowly turns to me and brushes my hair from my forehead. 'You all right, babe?' His eyes widen when he spies my bumped head. 'You're hurt. You've grazed yourself. Just here.' He strokes my forehead with the lightest touch, biting the inside of his cheek. 'You need to get that patched up ASAP.'

I give his knee a reassuring squeeze. 'I'm fine. Are you okay? Why did you slam on the brakes?' I can hear my heart hammering into my ribcage. It hasn't escaped me that the longer we sit here, the more chance we have of another car crashing into us.

'I saw something. A woman.' He scans the road around us again, his eyes lit with panic.

'A woman?'

'Yeah, in the middle of the road.'

'Oh, Peter. You're probably just tired. You've been so busy getting everything ready for the removal trucks. Let's just go.'

He shakes his head, pulling his arm away from my touch. I've never seen Peter scared before. It's like a layer of skin has been stripped away, and it's terrifyingly exposing. Plus, Peter is never wrong. If he says someone is out there, then someone is out there. Once again, I turn my attention to the empty road.

At this hour, most people are tucked up in bed, and it's hardly the weather for a nighttime jaunt. What did Peter see?

My deep breaths cloud the passenger-side window, and the sense of dread seems to turn the car from chariot to coffin.

A movement near my door catches my attention and I gasp. I go to wipe the condensation off the glass for a better view.

'Wait,' Peter warns, before pressing the button to lock the doors. They clunk in unison all around me. 'Just in case.'

But, his action has made me too scared to wipe the window and look out. Instead, I turn as my eyes follow the blurred movement as it shifts around to the back of the car and then floats past Peter's window.

'Holy shit,' Peter gasps. I twist around to see where he is looking.

A woman is now standing just inches from the car's bonnet, facing away from us. Her white hair lays dripping down her back, matted in thick knots. Her arms are bare, and her veins prominent under thin skin. She's wearing a pale yellow nightdress edged in fraying lace, which sticks to her skin, showcasing every bone in her emaciated body. I blush when I realise the material is practically see-through.

Her neck bends slowly until her head is almost perpendicular to her body and her ear is almost touching her shoulder, before she snaps her neck back upright at an incredible speed. I hold my breath, praying this is just a dream, but knowing deep down this is a real-life nightmare. My heart is screaming at me to go help her, but my fear digs its claws in, holding me back.

Ever brave, Peter makes the first move. 'Be right back,' he says, placing his hand on the door handle.

'Peter, wait!' I beg him, though I have no idea what I actually want to say. I want to tell him to stay here with me, but we can't just leave the poor woman out there.

Peter speaks my mind. 'I can't just leave her there, Jen. It's not like I can drive around her. She's right in the middle of the road.'

'No, I know. I just think I should go to her. You might frighten her.' Why did I say that? The last thing I want to do is head out there. But, in my gut, I know I'm right. She's incredibly vulnerable and it needs to be me.

'Why would I frighten her?' He sounds annoyed and pulls on the door handle. His door opens with a pop and a bonging noise erupts from the dashboard, alerting us that the engine is still running.

'She looks fragile. She might need a more feminine touch.' My hand reaches for the door handle, but I hesitate. I pray someone comes to get her before we need to take action.

He tuts at me. 'Just wait there, Jen-Jen.'

Before I have a chance to respond, he's gone, slamming his door shut behind him.

I nervously clasp my hands together as he approaches the woman, joining her in the beams of the headlights. He says something and her hands jerk upwards before flopping back to her sides. He repeats himself, his hands out in front of him in an attempt to show her he's harmless. He's pleading with her, but she just continues to twitch. It's like he's not even there.

Peter takes a tiny step back and scratches his head. I can tell he's getting frustrated; he always wrings his hands when he's annoyed, and he's doing it now. His teeth are showing in one corner of his mouth, and he throws a glance at me. I sink into my seat, feeling guilty for being in the warmth while they are out there in the sleet and rain.

To my astonishment, the woman slowly spins to face me, her bare feet dragging across the gravel. Her eyes are closed, and her lips are moving at an alarming speed. I realise she's muttering to herself.

What is this poor woman doing out here? Is she not cared for? It breaks my heart to think she's not being looked after and she's just wandering around to catch her death. If she actually did, would she even have anyone to mourn her?

I can only assume she's on the run from a care home that clearly needs to step up its security measures. Once I find out which one, I'll be damn sure to make a formal complaint. This is disgusting. Plus, her family deserves to know what kind of "care" they're potentially paying for.

I push away the distraction and refocus on the scene before me. Peter catches my eye and shrugs.

I need to help her. But, Peter told me to stay here. I sit on my hands.

A small *meow* sounds from the back seat.

'I know, boy. I'm worried, too.' I turn to face Oliver, tucked up in his new travel bag. His little white face peeps out at me, his green eyes wide with concern. My stomach sinks. My mum bought me Oliver as a Christmas present in a bid to cheer me up after Dad died. And now, Oliver has a heartbreaking knack of reminding me of her death, too.

Sensing my stress, he purrs at me and places a paw on the mesh.

'Okay, boy. I'll sort this out.' Emboldened by the act of feline kindness, I pull the door handle and head outside. The roar of the rain overwhelms me.

'I told you to stay in there!' Peter yells at me over the hammering rain. Thunder rumbles overhead, further away this time. I am immediately drenched and have to fight off the shivers.

'Sorry, honey! I just think I might have a better chance of helping her.' I gesture at the woman and her eyes suddenly fly open. They are bright blue, so bright they seem to glow, and I have to stop myself recoiling from the intensity of her stare.

Peter looks at me, then turns to look at the old lady, trying to decide his next move. He then throws his arms up in defeat and moves back, allowing me to nervously step closer to the old woman.

'Do you need help?' I stammer. It's a stupid thing to say; obviously she needs help. Obvious to everyone except herself, that is. I can't understand how she isn't shivering, standing dripping wet in this freezing temperature. Panic pulses in my throat as I realise we don't have long until she collapses.

The woman continues to stare at me, her eyes boring into my soul. I haven't yet seen her blink. She's still muttering under her breath, any sound she makes carried away by the wind.

'Come with us, we'll take you home.' I reach out to touch her arm and she jerks it away, the movement so quick I jump back in shock.

Her lips move more quickly now.

'Sorry.' I take a different, less direct approach. 'I'm Jen. This is my husband, Peter.' In my peripheral vision, I see Peter roll his eyes at my lack of action, but I force myself to keep looking at the woman. I need her to understand that we're not here to harm her. Maybe then, she'll trust us.

But, she just continues to stare. I shrug off my bright red coat and she watches as I approach her, holding my coat open. 'Here, take this.' She jerks her head to the side as I slip the coat over her shoulders, my trembling fingers almost dropping it into a puddle pooling at our feet.

'There you are. That's better, isn't it?' I smile at her, feeling like I have really made some progress. 'Would you like to come and sit in the car? It's warm. And you can meet my cat, Oliver – he's a friendly little thing. Would you like that?' At this, her lips stop moving and a smile almost forms.

But then, she goes back to mumbling.

I look to Peter for answers. 'Let's call an ambulance. Or the police!' he calls over. 'Have you got your phone on you?'

I check my trouser pockets and shake my head, and he nods towards the car before jogging back to it. I cast one more look at the woman before joining Peter.

He is already inside fumbling under his seat when I clamber into the passenger seat with a groan. I'm starting to get a whopping headache from when I bumped my head. 'Poor woman,' I say to him. I slam my door shut, relieved by the surrounding quiet of the car's interior.

'Damn right. She's bloody terrifying.'

I tap his arm. 'You can't say that! She's just a defenceless lady in need of help. Thank God we found her before she went over someone's bonnet.'

'Or the cold kills her off.' Giving up looking under his seat, Peter leans over me and starts rummaging around my feet. 'I can't find my damn phone; it must have fallen off the dashboard when I stopped the car. Have you got yours?'

At this moment, I remember where it is. 'Oh, crap, it's in my coat pocket.' Only I could be so stupid as to give a stranger my coat *and* my phone.

We both sit up straight. The hot air in the car has already begun turning our soaking wet clothes into condensation, coating the windows in a wet mist. Peter reaches forward and rubs a circle clear in the windshield, so we can see outside.

No. No, no, no.

I launch myself out of the car and whip my head around. Searching.

The woman has gone.

Nothing but my cherry-red coat remains, like a puddle of blood on the ground.

CHAPTER TWO

I run my fingers over the crushed velvet curtains. The pale pink fabric dances as I sweep them back to expose the room to the sun's warm rays. I sigh happily. It's finished. Our beautiful home is finished. All the effort has paid off – three months of hard work, and hours spent watching YouTube videos to learn the skills I needed to turn our modest little house into our very own palace. And my God, it has *so* been worth it.

I'm ashamed to say that when Peter first carried me over the threshold, I had to really mask my disappointment behind a huge smile and gushing compliments. In places, the carpets had worn away to the underlay, mould had blackened most walls, and the décor looked like something from a 1960s nightmare. When Peter had described our marital home, I had pictured something a little more ... comfortable. None of that matters anymore, though; the house now looks pristine, pretty, and perfect.

I head over to the fireplace and light a scented candle. I sniff the hints of sandalwood and vanilla and place the lighter on the bookshelf above our new TV. The living room is small, but functional. Two sofas line the walls, with cushions so plush you could dive into them and disappear. A thick, pink rug lays on the varnished wood flooring, adding an extra touch of luxury to the space. Bookshelves nestle in the alcoves on either side of the fireplace. I couldn't move anywhere without my book collection. The paint smell still lingers, symbolising our future of contentment and happiness, and I clap my hands to my mouth in excitement, squealing into my throat.

'Honey, I'm home!' Peter calls out from the front door. I cringe when he slams it shut behind him. Why can't he be more gentle?

'Hey, babe!' I call back, heading to the front of the house to greet him properly with a kiss.

He pulls me in and kisses me deeply, and I wrap my arms around his neck and sink into him. My aching muscles relax into his bulging ones. Eventually, he pulls away to take a breath. 'You're looking extra sexy today,' he tells me, kicking off his shoes and placing his bag on the floor by the stairs. He takes a step back to admire me in my dirty jeans, baggy T-shirt, and messy bun. I giggle and scoop up the shoes, placing them on his designated shoe rack. I'll take the bag upstairs later.

I follow him into the kitchen and watch him pour himself a glass of water, which he swallows in one gulp. His sleeves are pulled up, revealing his tanned forearms. He looks hot. Aroused, I press my lips together. 'How was work?' I ask him.

He nods, wiping his lips dry with his arm. 'It was okay. Put in a bid for a major project. I'm feeling hopeful.'

I press a hand to my lips. I can imagine him heading into his professional corporate job, sitting behind a huge desk, bossing his team around. He's so impressive. So inspirational. 'Did you like the lunch I made for you?'

He laughs. 'Oh, Jen-Jen, of course I did. You ask me that every day and the answer's always the same. You make incredible lunches.'

I blush. Am I nagging him? 'Sorry. I just want to do a good job.'

'Don't be silly. You just don't have to worry; you're perfect in every way.' He kisses the tip of my nose. 'I'm going for a shower. Be right back.'

In the three months since we married and moved in together, I have fallen in love with Peter more and more every day. I didn't even know that was possible. He's shown me a level of attentiveness I have struggled to get used to. When he's not at work, he spends all of his time cuddling me in front of a movie or massaging my feet while I read a book. He works so hard to provide for me. For us. And I will be forever grateful for that.

As he moves upstairs, his expensive aftershave lingers behind him and I draw it into me with a deep inhale. It causes my heart to pound in my chest so hard I swear I can see it. How did I get so lucky, falling for him? And for him to fall for me in return?

I potter around the kitchen, chucking some extra spice into the chilli because I know Peter likes food with a kick. I head into the dining room to check the table is set beautifully and pour Peter a glass of wine from the bottle that's been chilling in the fridge all day.

I hear the shower door slide open upstairs. Peter will be down soon, so I straighten his knife and fork on the table, then return to the kitchen to dish up dinner. He has told me before how he can only eat at the table; eating off your lap is lazy, apparently. I haven't told him this is the first time in my life I've had a dinner table to eat at.

Peter enters the kitchen in just a pair of shorts, his wet hair plastered against his face. He sniffs at the air with comical exaggeration. 'Dinner smells amazing.' He comes up behind me, wraps his arms around my waist, and nuzzles my ear.

I lean my head back to rest on his shoulder. 'Go and take a seat, I'll bring it over.' He taps my backside as he leaves the room with an exaggerated swish of his hips, making me laugh.

During dinner, Peter regales me with a story about a young woman mocked by one of the big bosses at work for falling pregnant and getting behind with her work because of chronic morning sickness. 'So, I told him to grow up. How dare he make her feel like crap for having a child? She's a woman, it's what they do. She shouldn't be punished for it.' He speaks with such passion, sloshing his wine around in his glass, and I love that. He's such a good guy.

After we've enjoyed our meal, I clean up in the kitchen while Peter relaxes in front of the TV. Peter works long hours. He often leaves the house at the crack of dawn and then doesn't come home until it's gone seven o'clock at night. The poor guy is exhausting himself, paying for the mortgage and indulging my newfound DIY hobby. Maybe now that the house is finished, he can pull back a bit. I doubt it though; Peter has such an admirable sense of responsibility. I imagine that's why he's paid so handsomely.

He's tucked up under a blanket when I walk into the living room holding another bottle of wine. I top up his glass and pour one for myself before sliding under the blanket with him. 'How was your day, Jen-Jen?'

I smile, grateful to finally be talking about the house. Sometimes I rabbit on about it too much and have to bite my tongue in case I bore him, but right now I am just so excited I'm fit to burst. And let's be honest – with no friends or family, I have little else to talk about. 'I think it's finished!' I tell him. 'I replaced the manky curtains in here today and touched up the scuffed skirting board in the spare bedroom. And that's it! Done!'

He smiles at me and looks at the curtains, noticing them for the first time. I press my lips together, nervous that he'll ask how much they cost (not that he has bothered about the price of things before). I can't shift the mismatch between this lavish life and the frugal one I have always experienced with Mum. With her, I was the provider, so taking from Peter now just feels so ... strange.

'You have done an incredible job. I can't get over how you have turned this house around. The perfect housewife.'

I wriggle into him a bit more, pressing myself up against his manliness. I relish his compliment and let my satisfaction swell inside me. There's just one thing that bothers me. 'I don't know what I'm going to do with myself now though. I'm going to be bored.'

He chuckles, pushing away my worry. 'You'll have to find a hobby besides wallpapering. Gardening, perhaps? It's a bit overgrown out there.'

I bristle. I spent three days out there last week, pulling out the weeds. I still need to plant some flowers, but it's a far cry from *overgrown*. 'Maybe I can get a part-time job, keep me busy?' I've had a job since I was fourteen, and as fun as it is to spend Peter's money, I hate not making my own. Don't get me wrong, I am so grateful to Peter for wanting to look after me, but I just feel a bit ... pointless. Especially now the house is complete.

'We've talked about this. You don't need to work. I've got the bills covered. Let me look after you, and you can do whatever you want.'

But, what I want is to work. I want to earn my own money instead of relying on Peter to drop some pocket money into my bank account, and the meagre inheritance from my mother was quickly swallowed up by decorating supplies. 'I appreciate that, I really do. I just think a job would be a good way to make friends around here.'

NANA   15

He runs his thumb over the back of my hand, making little figures of eight. 'Well, I will leave it up to you, but I just think there will be better, more fun ways to make friends. Plus, it'll really upset me if I can't provide for you.' He touches my chin and lifts my face to meet his. Our lips touch and the conversation ends.

***

When we finish in the bedroom, we both lean back against the head-board, sweat beading on Peter's forehead, my breathing laboured. Sex with Peter is always so ... vigorous. He likes to dominate, and I release myself to his every whim. It's exhilarating, yet so exhausting. I get up for a glass of water to soothe my throat, leaving Peter dozing in bed.

When I return from the kitchen, I linger at the other end of the corridor, outside the spare bedrooms. The larger of the two is decorated with Minecraft memorabilia. On one wall, I've stencilled a boxy-looking figure the internet told me would be favoured by a Minecraft fan, and Minecraft pictures cover the other walls. All the shelves are stacked with comic books and graphic novels that I hope a ten-year-old boy will like.

'He's going to love it, you know?' Peter creeps up behind me and presses his hands on my shoulders. Tomorrow, Peter's son, Max, is coming to visit for the first time. Despite having been with Peter for eleven months, I am yet to meet his son, and I am ashamed to admit that I'm absolutely dreading it.

Nerves weigh in my stomach. Even if he likes the room, that doesn't mean he will like *me*. I just pray that the room is a good start. I keep my worries to myself though, as I don't want to worry Peter. I don't want him to think I'm not happy with the situation. I just want Max to like me, but how can a child warm to the woman who took his daddy away?

When I think back to how Peter and I met, shame mingles with the happiness I want to feel and it drags me down into a pit of misery. When Peter first walked into the bar, my eyes were immediately drawn to him. He walked in with such a swagger, a smile plastered across his face, and his seductive eyes looked me up and down with approval. He winked at me and that was it – I fell hook, line, and sinker.

'Well, aren't you something special,' he said to me, leaning over the bar to get a bit closer. I got a whiff of his aftershave, and I breathed it in deeply, longing to soak myself in him. Love at first sight felt like a foolish notion before I met Peter. It always seemed too "Disney". But, right there and then, I fell head over heels in love.

It was just a shame he was married. Three weeks later, his wife Sara found a text from me on his phone and kicked him out. It was the best thing that could have happened. After that, it took six months for the divorce to come through. Six long months of waiting for Peter to leave his home with her. It was an agonising wait, but he had to remain loyal to his Max, a trait I can only admire. Three days after the decree absolute came through, we were married.

Then, Peter jumped into action to buy us a home together. My love for him finally felt secure. I felt at peace. We were meant to be together and now we can be, without having to hide. Without having to feel immense shame every time his phone rings. Without me having to kiss him goodbye while wondering if his wife is doing the exact same thing when he leaves their home.

Now, there is just the matter of Max to handle. It feels silly, worrying about a ten-year-old boy, but I really want him to like me. If he doesn't, will Peter second-guess our relationship? Will I still be the image of perfection he fell in love with? Well, making Max's bedroom as homely as possible is a good place to start. And that's perfect. I hope.

I turn to my right to face the smaller spare bedroom, and sigh. Peter follows my gaze to look at the blank, pale yellow space. I am itching to stencil something cute along the skirting board, but it feels a little too premature. 'It won't be long until we start a family of our own,' I say, trying to coax a definitive answer out of Peter. He's already promised it's happening; I just need to know *when*. I need a goal to get excited about.

Peter lets go of my shoulders. 'Soon, Jen-Jen. Let's just settle in here a bit first, yeah? Plus, we need to get Max on board.'

He's right, of course. The last thing that young lad needs is a baby sibling thrust upon him. I can wait a few months. If there is one thing on our side, it's age. Peter might be fourteen years older than me, but he is very much fully functional and there is plenty of life in him yet. Being only thirty myself, we're in a safe position. We have time.

Peter is right – we need to take things slowly. I just need to learn how to be more patient.

CHAPTER THREE

Peter is pacing around the living room, his anxiety feeding my stress. For the third time, I rearrange the doughnuts I've placed on the coffee table. Will Max like jam or custard? I spread them out, so he can see his options better.

They're ten minutes late. Maybe they've hit traffic or something. The roads on the other side of the city can be terrible at this time on a Saturday morning, with everyone rushing to the shops. Or, perhaps their route has taken them past Asda; that's pretty much always grid-locked.

Or, maybe Sara is trying to wind me up. She's playing games with me. I take a deep breath. Getting upset isn't going to help. Neither is wringing my hands together, so I pull them apart and force them down by my sides.

Peter has barely said a word to me this morning. I think his nerves are eating him up and I haven't pushed him to open up to me. He'll talk when he's ready. When he sees me and Max getting along, I'm sure he'll be full of things to say.

Finally, a car pulls up outside the house: a BMW soft-top. The driver's door opens and ridiculously long legs emerge. Sara's wearing the most beautiful heels, black patent with delicate straps. I glance down at the slippers I am wearing and kick them off behind the sofa. At least my toenails are painted. I catch Peter's eye and he throws me what I think is supposed to be an encouraging smile, but it's more of a terrified grimace. I return the smile, keeping my face composed, praying my calm exterior will give him a slight sense of peace. The doorbell rings.

'Wait here a minute,' Peter says. 'Oh, and Jen – whatever you hear, Sara is full of shit, yeah?' He rushes out to greet our guests. I stand awkwardly in the middle of the living room, waiting for Peter to usher them both inside.

'Hey, how you doing, mate?' I hear Peter ask. I'm assuming he is talking to Max, but I don't hear a response. Shamefully, Peter has only seen Max a handful of times since meeting me. It wasn't a conscious decision; time just slipped by. Guilt gnaws at me. How much has my existence hurt this young boy? I *must* make amends, and I am scared it's not going to be easy.

'Thanks for bringing him over,' Peter says.

'No bother. I was over this way, anyway,' Sara says, her voice that sexy kind of husky. Why was she over this way? Thistlewood is in the middle of nowhere, and isn't even en route anywhere. I'd put money on her coming here to be nosy.

'You're looking really good,' Peter says. But to whom?

There's a moment's silence, but then Sara replies, 'Well, a lot of things have improved since you left, Peter.'

'Right, well, I'll bring Max back tomorrow,' he tells her, sensibly ignoring her cutting remark. I breathe a sigh of relief, inwardly thanking Peter for not inviting her in. One meet-and-greet is enough for today.

Peter and I spoke about this last night. We agreed it's best I don't meet Sara too soon. I need to focus my efforts on welcoming Max, and he feels that Sara might derail me. I couldn't agree with him more.

'Aren't you going to show me around your new love pad?' I hear high heels click along the wooden hallway floor. My heart sinks. She's coming in. I straighten my back and squeeze my eyes shut as I wait for Peter to stop her. He mumbles something under his breath, and I wring my hands together again. *Please, Peter, don't let me down.*

The living room door nudges open and I spring back, planting a smile on my face, hoping it looks genuine. Peter appears first. He's white as a sheet and refuses to meet my eye. He mouths "sorry" at me as he enters. I shrug, letting him know it's all okay. It's not, of course, but he doesn't need to feel bad. This isn't his fault.

Max follows Peter in next, his head down. All I can see of him are blonde curls. His movements are sluggish and awkward. I say "hello", but he doesn't even acknowledge my presence and helps himself to a custard doughnut before throwing himself onto the sofa. I swell when I see him wearing a Minecraft T-shirt. This might be okay after all. He just needs to see his new room.

'And you must be Jennifer,' says Sara, entering the room. She holds out a manicured hand. I take it and give it a little shake before swiping my hand behind my back, ashamed of the dry skin and broken nails.

I give her what I hope is my warmest smile. 'Please, call me Jen,' I tell her.

Sara raises an eyebrow at me, and I find myself inwardly cowering from her gaze. She screams success. Her blonde hair is highlighted with golden streaks, and her designer clothes are practical yet stylish. Her jeans hug her slim legs, and her blouse is bright white, unbuttoned to reveal a hint of cleavage and a classy gold necklace.

I pull my cardigan tightly around myself and wrap my arms around my waist. Why did Peter pick me? Why choose a Burger King when he already had Wagyu steak? Tears sting the back of my eyes and I blink furiously to push them away.

'Ready to play step-mum, Jennifer?' Sara says with a glint in her eye.

My mouth bobs open while I try to think of a response. Peter shifts from one foot to the other. 'I am certainly ready to make a new friend,' I say.

Peter grins from ear to ear and Sara cocks her head to the side. I think I said the right thing. Even Max peeks at me through the same hazel eyes as his daddy's, licking sugar off his fingers.

'Well, good luck with that.' She turns to face Peter, her chest inches from his. 'You always struggled with friendships, didn't you, Peter? Just not good with people.' She stares at him, straight in the eye. Peter just shifts from one foot to the other again, biting the inside of his cheek. She chuckles and turns away. 'Right, well, I had better go. Max, you going to be okay with your dad?' She kneels to face Max and strokes his hair away from his worried face. 'You've got this, little man.' Her tenderness warms me to her, a little bit.

Max nods, but he doesn't look okay. He looks like he'd rather be left with Pennywise than me.

Peter steps in to break the tension. 'We'll have fun, I promise. And you'll see your mum tomorrow.'

Max nods and looks up at his dad. 'I'll be okay, Mum,' he says with forced confidence.

His mum, satisfied, nods and stands up. 'He's got his mobile if he needs me,' she tells Peter, turning her back to me. 'He can call me any time. My phone will be on *loud*.'

Peter rolls his eyes; I share his sentiment. This is all a bit over the top. Peter is his dad, after all. Max will be fine. But, I remain still and silent, reluctant to be drawn into the situation. I would give anything to spend just ten minutes with my dad. Sara doesn't know how lucky she is to have two competent parents for her precious boy. Sara ruffles Max's hair before leaving without so much as a "goodbye" to me and Peter. I exhale through pursed lips, relieved to have that awkward meeting over and done with.

There's a moment of silence while we adjust to the present situation. Then, Peter and Max run off towards Peter's office where the Xbox is set up, taking the plate of doughnuts with them. 'Can you bring us each a drink please, love?' Peter calls out to me as he passes. I watch them disappear. If they're in there, it means I can spend some alone time making them a nice lunch. I am unsure what Max likes, so I've stocked the kitchen with a bit of everything.

After I switch on the oven to preheat, I head through the dining room to the office, with two massive strawberry milkshakes in those charming tall glasses you get in American diners. Peter and Max are already absorbed in a game, their characters donning military uniforms and firing huge guns. Boys are odd.

I hope we have a girl to balance things out a bit. It'll be nice to have someone I can pamper – French braid her hair, paint her nails. I would take her shopping for party dresses and sparkly shoes. A warmth spreads through me as I return to the kitchen and push the chicken bites and potato wedges into the oven.

Peter keeps telling me to wait a little while before we start trying for a baby, but I get the feeling we can't be far off now. The house is finished. The Sara-and-Max hurdle has been jumped. Peter is doing so incredibly well at work. What's stopping us?

Oliver meows from the breakfast bar and I reach out to tickle the back of his ear. He pushes his head into my hand, his purrs vibrating against my skin. 'I know, boy. We've struck gold here, haven't we?' I run one hand down Oliver's back, and place the other on my tummy.

All is well. Everything is going to be just perfect.

CHAPTER FOUR

I'm bored. I have been trying to read for the last hour, but my attention is constantly drawn to Peter's office where he and Max are still battling on some rubbish computer game. Sharing Peter with Max is the right thing to do, and I have had more than my fair share of Peter's attention lately, so I am trying to keep out, but this isn't how I envisaged today going. I haven't even had the chance to get to know Max; to win him over. But, Peter knows best. If Max spends more quality time with his dad, he'll no doubt feel more secure in his relationship with him, so then he's surely more likely to warm to me. That's what I keep telling myself, anyway.

The doorbell rings, making my eyebrows crease. Oh, please don't let that be Sara coming back. Did Max text her asking her to pick him up? Is he not having a good time? I wait for Peter to go and answer the door, but gunfire continues to pour out of the room next to me, so I head to the front entrance. I see two figures standing behind the frosted glass and I pray they're not here to try and recruit me for whatever cause they're fighting. I've noticed an increasing number of placards in the village lately – something about a railway line.

'Hiya!' says a friendly voice as I pull the door open. An older couple are standing on my doorstep, both smiling at me with a kind warmth. 'We wanted to welcome you to the village. We would have come sooner, but we've been on holiday.'

The woman in front of me greets me with a genuine smile, her large eyes sparkling, her lips full and painted a garish shade of pink. Her full cheeks have a ruddy glow to them, which pairs well with her flowery dress. Standing next to her is a man I assume is her husband. His hairline is receding slightly and he's wearing brown corduroy trousers that make him appear older than his fit physique suggests. It's clear that this man takes working out seriously; between his muscular build and the thick hair poking out of his cream shirt, he resembles a gorilla. Their smiles are so friendly, their demeanour so easy. They're holding hands, too; it's so sweet. Having been preoccupied with the house, other than the odd smile and wave with various neighbours, this is the first chance I have had to speak to people in the community.

'Hi, come in!' I lead them into the living room and they settle themselves on the sofa underneath the window. 'Can I get you anything? Tea? Coffee?'

'Oh, no, love. We won't stop for long. We just wanted to give you this.' The man hands me a deceptively heavy box he's had tucked under his arm. I pull the cardboard lid off and gasp. Inside is a lovely stone Buddha figurine. His eyes are closed and he is resting his hands on crossed legs. He's the image of serenity.

'We're not religious, but we thought he might bring you a little peace and tranquillity. Well, that's what the website says, anyway,' the man says with a small smile.

'I love it!' I tell them truthfully. He belongs in the garden, but for now I place him with a clunk on the fireplace, where he sits smiling up at me. He really is lovely. What a thoughtful gift.

'I'm Greg, by the way, and this is my wife, Erin,' the man tells me, pulling his wife towards him.

'I'm Jen. How lovely for you to stop by.' I perch on the arm of the sofa by the door. 'Have you lived in Thistlewood for long?'

'Our whole lives,' Greg says with pride. 'We both went to the primary school on Vicarage Lane. It's where we met, actually. Though we didn't get romantically involved until high school.'

I simper. I love a romantic tale. 'And you've been loved-up ever since? How lovely.'

Erin nods. 'Yeah, poor bugger. He's stuck with me now.'

I try to tell them that can't possibly be true, but they laugh, brushing away my unnecessary reassurance.

'Have you met your next-door neighbours yet?' Greg asks me.

'Not yet. I have been over a few times to introduce myself, but no one was in. They must have just been busy.'

'Ah, Kay sure is a busy lady. She was probably at one of her many jobs or rushing the kids around to whoever will take them.'

I note that they don't mention a dad and file it away in my things to remember, so that I don't embarrass myself when I do finally meet this Kay lady. 'How many kids does she have?' I have heard screaming and laughter next door. They sing a lot, too. They sound like a lovely family.

'Two girls. Or three, if you want to count ...'

Erin nudges Greg. 'Be nice,' she mutters.

Greg just nods. Though my curiosity is piqued, I don't want to appear nosy. Maybe Kay had a miscarriage or something. It isn't my place to ask, so I swiftly change the subject. 'So, what is there to do around here? It feels incredibly quiet.'

'Not a lot, to tell the truth. But, don't worry, I'm sure you'll be kept on your toes,' says Greg.

Again, Erin throws him a glance, then changes the subject. I feel like Greg is the guy to talk to if I want to really get to know people. I make a mental note to try and talk to him alone.

'There's the community centre,' Erin tells me. 'All sorts goes on there. Yoga, craft nights, discos. There are a number of fundraising events throughout the year, too, like the Christmas Fair in December. You should speak to Gill, who owns the place; you know, get involved.'

I nod emphatically. 'Thanks! I'll do that.'

'Or, find Laura. I'm surprised she hasn't found you first, really. She'll give you a rundown of events and happenings. She enjoys a good gossip.'

Greg cuts in. 'Oh, that's true that. Just take what she says with a pinch of salt, if you know what I mean.'

I have no idea what he means, and I shift uncomfortably. Is Laura someone to be wary of?

'Is it just you here?' Greg asks me. He's just being polite; you can't fail to notice the raucous gunfire coming from the next room.

'My husband is in his office,' I admit.

'Oh, my goodness! What's his profession? 007?'

I laugh politely, not quite appreciating the joke, and say, 'He's spending quality time with his son, playing games. But, he should come and say hello. I'll go and get him.'

I slap my knees and go to stand up, but Erin reaches over and touches my hand. 'Oh, no, darling. Don't interrupt them. We really can't stay. We just wanted to come and meet you and welcome you to the village.'

Greg's eyebrows lift. '*His* son. None of your own, then?'

Erin snaps her head around to glare at him.

I don't mind the intrusive question. 'No.' *Not yet*, I want to add. Once again, excitement tickles me as I think about the baby I will soon be clutching to my chest, showing off to whoever asks.

'Oh, well – if you want our advice, don't wait too long, like we did. Ain't that right, Erin?'

Erin blushes, but doesn't take her eyes off me. I see the sadness in them and wish I could reach over and hug her pain away. 'That's right,' she says, putting a stop to the conversation. 'Well, if there is anything you need, anything at all, just come and knock on our door. We live in the thatched cottage by the duck pond.'

I know exactly which house they mean; I admire that building every time I drive past it. Surrounded by high hedges, it's shrouded in mystery, but you can *just* glimpse flashes of colour from the rose garden through the gate. It's like something out of a Disney film.

'Thank you so much. I'll pop over some time, I'm sure.' Having people in the village I can say hello to feels like a massive weight off my shoulders. For the first time since being here, I realise how lonely I have been feeling, especially now that I've finished decorating the house.

We head into the hall and Erin pauses by the side table to pull me close for a brief hug. Her ample bum bumps into the key bowl with a clatter. She's all warm and soft … like my mum used to be. 'Don't be a stranger,' she whispers in my ear. 'And don't believe everything you hear. People 'round here are a little … opinionated.'

CHAPTER FIVE

I can't help feeling a bit annoyed with Peter. He's barely said a word to me since Max arrived yesterday. Last night, after giving me a rundown of his day, he made love to me, but it was quick and aggressive. His satisfaction made him fall asleep before he tended to my needs, leaving me tossing and turning in frustration.

I got up especially early this morning, to warm some croissants in the oven and present various jams and marmalades in really cute jars. But, when they both came downstairs, Max didn't even throw me a glance and Peter swiftly kissed me on the cheek. Neither acknowledged the food I had prepared before heading straight back into the office to fire up the Xbox.

I try to make sense of it all. I bet Peter doesn't want to show me too much affection as he's still trying to win Max over, and public displays of affection with his new wife are hardly a good way to do that. Once Peter is back in Max's good books, it will be my turn. Then, once Peter has Max's ear, he can put in a good word for me. At least I assume that's Peter's plan. He hasn't exactly told me what he's thinking. I'll have a chat with him tonight, once he's taken Max back to Sara's.

I'm upstairs putting on mascara when I hear the front door slam shut. Peter is taking Max to buy some new school shoes, leaving me alone to nip around downstairs and collect their plates and glasses. It would have been nice if he'd said goodbye.

I hate to be a bitch, but I can't wait to get our house back tonight. I feel like a stranger wandering around the rooms I have spent so much time making mine. Because of the prenup, legally the house is Peter's, so I can't seem to settle here. And now that Max has come along, I feel more alien than ever, and I long to spend some time making memories with my gorgeous husband.

Feeling stir-crazy, I scoop up my keys and head outside. I hear somebody shriek next door, followed closely by an explosion of laughter. The sound of a happy family. I contemplate going around to introduce myself, but I'm in a bit of a mood and not in the right frame of mind to make friends, so I head for my car instead. I'll go and grab some yeast and pizza toppings from the supermarket – cooking always soothes me, and it'll be nice to reconnect with Peter tonight over a glass of wine and a good meal.

Asda is a fifteen-minute drive down the winding roads that led us here the night we moved in. As I round the bend tucked between high hedgerows, my mind flashes back to the old woman we almost crashed into *that* night. I can see her so vividly, standing there – pale, ghostly, in desperate need of food, warmth, and family. I wish we could have helped her.

For days after that incident, I scoured the local news in the vain hope I would hear about a lost lady, now found and safe. Only, that didn't happen. Did she go home before it became newsworthy? Or did nobody care enough to alert anyone? In that case, was she ever found? Sadness wells inside me. Imagine growing old and having no one to care for you. No one to keep you safe. It's truly heartbreaking.

My focus jerks back to the present as I almost veer off the road. I hadn't realised the bend in the road was that sharp, and my heart is pounding in my head as I regain control of the steering wheel. I breathe deeply, finding some semblance of calm inside me, and I try to remain positive and assume she's okay. Maybe she often goes for a nighttime stroll; maybe she's made of harder stuff than my thirty-year-old pathetic self. I mean, I can't even get out of the bath without shivering like a plate of jelly, whereas she clearly felt nothing while standing in freezing temperatures.

I slow down as I approach the corner where we encountered her. I wince. An irrational reaction, I know, but I can't help it. I don't want to hit someone. There's no one there. Just the sunshine catching through the bushes, giving the road a striped effect.

I take another deep breath and sink into a comfort that springtime always brings me. New beginnings are afoot and it is truly beautiful here. Fields roll out around me, the various shades of green and a myriad of textures looking so inviting, so clean. A hint of manure makes my nose crinkle, in a good way; not in a vomit-splattered-path way that I used to experience on a Sunday morning outside my old Birmingham apartment. Yes, I think I can be very happy here.

All thoughts of the old woman leave me as I find a parking space in Asda. It's Sunday lunch time, so quite busy as people make a last-minute mad rush to buy veg for their Sunday roasts. Inside the supermarket, I'm pondering over various types of flour when I feel a tap on my shoulder.

'Excuse me for interrupting, but are you the lady who has moved into the old Dutton house?' I turn to face a stunning woman who is absolutely glowing. She's gorgeous! My face must express my confusion. 'Sorry, fourteen Cedar Grove,' she says. She's smiling at me, eagerly, like she can't wait to hear my answer.

'Yes?' I say, half-asking in my confusion. She's standing so close, I can feel her breath on my cheek, and I take a step back.

'Sorry, darling, I didn't mean to startle you.' She laughs a tinkly laugh. 'I've seen you coming and going around the village and rumour has it you moved into the Dutton house. Forgive me, I'm such a nosy monkey at times.'

Her blonde hair is immaculately curled, and her fake eyelashes curl up over her perfectly blended eyeshadow. Her teal, mid-length dress skims over her perfect curves. Her low heels match her outfit perfectly. She reeks money, but her smile screams kindness. I don't know whether to feel intimidated or warmed. I frown. 'The Duttons lived there before us?'

'Oh, yeah – Steve and Priya. Nice couple. She was a beautiful lady. It was such a shame when they left, but with village politics the way they are, it's hardly surprising.'

I imagine she is talking about the placards and posters I have seen everywhere. They're plastered to every lamppost, every window, every tree. From what I gather, there is a proposal to build a railway connection near the village. Is that why the Duttons left? I make a mental note to talk to Peter about it. He'll know if we have something to worry about.

She looks genuinely sad, but her sad gaze is swiftly replaced by delight when she extends her hand to me. 'I'm Laura, by the way.' I take her hand and give it a shake. It feels limp in mine, and I worry I might snap her dainty bones. 'I live near the school. Up the hill a little.'

My jaw drops open. There is only one house by the school. Laura lives in Thistlewood Manor, a vast building whose opulence mocks us peasants at the bottom of the hill. I'm in awe and immediately less comfortable in her presence.

'So, how are you settling in? Is there anything you need?'

'We've settled in just fine. Thistlewood is such a beautiful place.'

'It most definitely is. When everyone is behaving, anyway.' She nods vigorously. 'And who's *we*? Do you have a family?'

'It's just me and my husband,' I say. I don't tell her about Max. It feels too complicated for a quick chat with a stranger in the supermarket.

She gasps and presses a manicured hand to her chest. 'Is your husband the one in the Mercedes? The dishy one with floppy hair?' She runs her hand over her face, mimicking Peter's thick, dark hair.

I bristle. I'm not sure how I feel about someone calling my husband *dishy*. 'That's the one,' I tell her. *And he's all mine*, I long to add. Instead, I attempt to paint a picture of nonchalance on my face. 'What about you? Are you married?'

'Oh, yes!' Laura gushes. 'I'm married to Harry. Like your husband, he's the classic tall, dark, and handsome. Wears suits, usually Versace. He spends a lot of time on the oil rigs being the big boss, so you might not have seen him yet. He's a busy man. Most of the time, it's just me and Elijah, he's nine.'

Her eyes light up at the mention of her son. A mother's love is a beautiful thing. A smile sweeps across my face in anticipation of Peter's and my future baby, and I give the trolley handle a squeeze.

'Have you met anyone in the village yet? You seem to be keeping to yourself a bit.'

'I guess I have a little, but I've just been busy,' I say. I feel silly about my lack of friends. 'Greg and Erin popped around to introduce themselves. Do you know them? They seemed lovely.'

Laura's smile freezes, but her eyes sparkle with distaste. 'Yes, I've known them for years. I don't have much to do with them, though – and here's hoping it stays that way.' She coughs. 'And what about work? Or are you a fellow lady of leisure?'

Of course Laura is a lady of leisure. Good for her, if it makes her happy, but it's not a lifestyle for me. 'I will be looking for work. I just haven't had time yet.' It's the truth; I haven't had a spare second to search the job vacancy sites. But also, when I think about job-hunting, Peter's words bounce around my head. He's so eager for me to put my feet up and relax, and let him pay the bills, which puts me off looking. I imagine he's just thinking ahead. Securing a job just before we try for a baby is hardly practical, but I've never *not* worked. Sitting around just feels so ... lazy. And if I'm honest, lonely.

'That's incredible. Well done, you. What kind of work are you looking for?'

'I'm a bookkeeper,' I say proudly. I passed my exams after I left school, and I have worked for all kinds of businesses and sole traders. I love my job. Now that I don't have to moonlight as a server behind a bar for extra cash, I can really relax into it, too. Maybe that's why I am so keen to get back to work.

'You are a clever girl, aren't you?'

Girl? Laura can only be five or six years older than me. I smile at the compliment, though.

'Well, I'll let you head off. How about we swap numbers?'

'Yeah, sure.' I whip out my phone and take her number before calling her to return the favour. Laura seems lovely – she oozes kindness and despite having differing opinions about working, I think we can be friends.

***

Peter's car is parked in the driveway when I arrive home, and I tingle with the familiar sense of excitement that washes over me every time I get to see him.

As I exit my car, laden with bags, I hear music blasting from next door and I frown. I'm not one to complain about noise, especially in the middle of the day, but that doesn't mean I want to listen to some 1940s swing music through my walls. Their car isn't in the drive, however, so I assume it's one of the children. Not one to cause a scene, I shuffle inside my own house without so much as glancing next door.

The second I step over the threshold, Peter pulls me in for a lingering kiss. I lean into him for a fraction of a second before remembering. 'Max!' I tell him. 'We can't do this in front of him!'

'He's not here,' Peter mumbles into my mouth, pulling me closer.

I let him kiss me, my mind distracted by thoughts of his son. This feels so wrong. 'Where is he?' I ask, when Peter pulls away to kiss my neck.

'Back home. Sara met us in town for a coffee and she took him home from there.'

My eyes widen. Peter's kisses move over my chest and he cups my breast in his hand. He met his ex for a coffee? I was under the impression he was going to drop Max off at Sara's later. He said he didn't even plan on getting out of the car, so that he didn't have to face her. Drop and go.

Peter is too busy to notice my dismay as his mouth continues south. I try to push all thoughts of Peter's ex-wife out of my mind and get lost in the moment I have craved since Max walked through the door. But, Sara lingers in my mind like a nasty shadow.

CHAPTER SIX

The week passes by in a blur. Feeling bored and in need of a new project, I decide to throw myself into finishing the garden.

The apartment I lived in with Mum didn't have a garden. The only outdoor space was a tiny balcony overlooking the rubbish-strewn courtyard four floors below. I used to sit out there on a regular basis, savouring whatever sunshine could fight through the gaps in the tower block flats. But, then Mum became more and more of a danger to herself, and I had to keep the door locked to prevent her getting out and accidentally throwing herself over the ledge.

I truly loved my mum. I really did, and it kills me to say it, but there's a little part of me that's relieved she's gone. After Dad died, she lived a miserable life, staring into the bottom of a bottle. Over the space of a few years, her reliance grew from one sip to a bottle every night. A habit that resulted in her death. I sometimes wonder if her death gave her a chance to move away from all that, onto a new beginning.

My dad died when I was fourteen years old. My memories of him are fleeting and the older I get, the harder it is for me to grasp onto them. From then on, Mum slipped further away from me, piece by piece. The change was so slow to start with that it was hard for me to notice at first.

I cleared up after her. Held her up when she couldn't stand. Went to every hospital appointment with her. I cared for her – emotionally, physically, and, as I got older, financially. I wouldn't change that for the world. She was my mum and I love her. *Loved* her.

I just wish I got it right. Her bursts of anger made me live on tenterhooks. I was tired and so absorbed by her pain and I didn't have anyone else. I just didn't get the opportunity to meet people, and certainly had no strength to let people get close.

Then, just a few months after Mum died, Peter came along and offered me a new start. He was sunshine through the darkest clouds and all I wanted was to cling onto him until the agony of grief released its grip on me. And he let me, without complaint.

There was just the minor problem of the wife to solve first. I needn't have worried, though; one sniff of an affair and she gave Peter his marching orders. He would have left her for me before then, but he was understandably too devoted to Max – another reason I fell in love with him. Now, his ex is out of the picture and my mourning no longer absorbs me. Everything is finally perfect. Or at least, it was. Before the ex-wife came sniffing around.

I pull my hands out of the soil, kneel back onto my heels, and squeak with pride. I have spent the week filling flower pots and baskets, creating new flower beds, and tidying up around the edges. I have planted a myriad of varieties, colour-coding each bed. I have attached trellis to the brickwork for the newly-planted rose bushes to travel up as they grow.

It's going to be glorious. A creation of blood, love, and sweat. I can just imagine sitting out here in the summer, Peter tending to a barbeque with a cold beer in his hand. I'll be sunbathing with a book by the apple tree in the centre of the garden, my belly starting to swell, growing our baby.

I push myself up. My tongue feels like sandpaper and I'm a bit wobbly when I stand, so I head into the kitchen for a much-needed glass of juice. The kitchen is so much cooler than outside, and I take pleasure in dipping my head into the fridge to cool down. I pull the chicken out of the drawer and set to chopping it for dinner. Peter loves my Thai green curry and as it's Friday, I want to make a feast for him to celebrate the beginning of the weekend. I have even bought him that Thai beer he likes.

I lose myself in preparing dinner, singing as I work. Alexa has chosen some banging tunes, and I am singing along to the Backstreet Boys when a movement in the garden catches my eye. It came from behind the washing line at the back of the garden. Perhaps it was just the wind catching the towels drying on the line.

No, it was something else. I'm sure of it. Something bigger.

I stand on tip-toes, trying to see behind the sea of blue towels, but it's useless. My view is blocked.

The back door isn't locked, and it groans when I push it open and step into my gardening crocs. The air feels thick and cloying, and I have to breathe deeply to work it into my lungs. Only the sound of birdsong greets me. All is quiet next door, and we're too far from the main road for traffic sounds to drift over. Will it be this quiet once they have built the railway? I approach the swaying towels and make a mental note to soften them in the drier before I go to bed.

Then, I see her. She's squatting in front of my newly-planted crocuses, her scraggly white hair falling down her back. She's mumbling something, like she's telling something off.

I call out. 'Excuse me. Can I help you?' My blood runs cold through my veins. There's something odd about this (other than the fact she is trespassing).

She sits bolt upright, still not turning to face me. Her entire body is rigid, like a corpse. The skin on the back of her neck is wrinkled, her veins prominent under her white skin.

It can't be …

'Can I help you?' I repeat.

Is this … *her*? Is this the woman we nearly ran over when we moved here?

She doesn't move, so I step closer. If it is the woman we found on the road that night, she needs help. I need to take her home before she wanders back onto the road.

Slowly, she turns to face me, still squatting down in front of the flower bed.

I gasp. 'It *is* you …'

Flashes of memory fly past. The same pale, bright eyes are looking back at me, open wide.

She looks into my eyes and her jaw jerks from side to side. Is she … chewing? I spy a sprinkling of purple petals on her chin and a stem hangs out of her mouth, leaving a trail of dirt on her chin. She's eating my crocuses!

I step over to her and reach out, hesitating for a nanosecond before taking her arm. She doesn't react – not even a flex of a muscle.

'Where do you live? Let me take you home.' Pity drips from my voice. This is someone's relative, obviously sick and just free to do as she pleases.

I tap my pocket to retrieve my phone, but realise I've left it on the kitchen worktop and I sigh with frustration. I really need to learn to keep it on me.

'Come inside. I'll get you a nice cup of tea,' I say. Although, maybe a hot drink isn't a good idea. What if she spills it on herself? 'Or a glass of juice? I made some banana bread yesterday, do you like banana bread?'

I'm rambling, desperately searching for the words that will make this woman come inside. She brings a handful of petals to her wrinkled mouth and pushes them inside like she's snacking on popcorn.

I help her stand up and give her a gentle tug towards the house, but she tugs back, pulling us further away from my goal. I don't know what to do. We can't just stand here. Peter won't be home until much later, and the evening is fast approaching.

'Wait here,' I tell her. I won't take my eyes off her. She's not escaping this time.

I dash inside, twisting my neck back to keep the woman in my peripheral vision. She stands still, staring at me, as if *I'm* the crazy one.

My phone is on the table in the hall next to the key bowl, and I fly across the kitchen to fetch it.

I return to the kitchen and look out the window to see a flurry of blue zoom across the garden. She's running off with my laundry, a towel flapping manically above her head.

'Hey!' I call out, chasing after her. 'Come back!'

Before I can catch up, she's out of the side gate, letting it slam behind her. The latch has slipped down, impeding my advance.

'Hang on!' I yell out, running up the driveway. But, my call is wasted. She's gone again. There are a few trees lining the roadside, so I jog up the road a little to see if she's hiding behind one. But, she has disappeared.

How does this woman keep disappearing like this? I trudge back into my garden and look at the washing line, scratching my head.

***

I spend the evening feeling dishevelled and missing Peter terribly. Eight o'clock rolls by, then nine o'clock. There's still no sign of Peter. I knew he was going for a couple of drinks after work, but he said he'd be home for a "late dinner". Surely 9:20 is too late for even a "late dinner". I have been keeping the curry warm, but it's now at that point where I am seriously doubting its edibility.

By the time his taxi pulls up outside our house an hour later, I am wringing my hands and pacing around the living room. I've been going out of my mind, imagining him lying in a ditch somewhere, sans wallet and phone. Why else would he not pick up when I tried to call him? Who is he drinking with, anyway? He hasn't actually said.

He doesn't say a word when he walks in the door. He glances at me, looking sheepish. At least he's got the gall to look ashamed.

I try to swallow my annoyance and worry. 'Good day?' I snap, failing miserably.

'Oh, Jen-Jen, don't be like that. You know I have to smooth-talk people to get the job done. It pays the bills, doesn't it?'

He's right, of course. A lot of Peter's success comes from his ability to network and pull key business contacts into the company. I swallow my annoyance and take a deep breath. 'Of course, honey. I've just missed you today, that's all.'

His shoulders visibly drop when he realises he's not in the dog-house. 'Well then, seeing as you asked, I've had a great day. That project I was telling you about has been given the green light.'

I have no idea what he's talking about, but he looks so pleased with himself that I wrap my arms around his neck anyway. 'That's such good news, babe. Well done.' He kisses me on the tip of my nose. 'I'll serve dinner. You must be starving.' My stomach rumbles as I say this. I have waited for Peter to come home to eat and I'm desperate for food.

'Oh, no, I ate already. I'm going to have a shower.'

He jogs up the stairs, taking two at a time. I watch him go, my fingers squeezing into fists by my side. I have been looking forward to seeing him all day. Being apart from him physically hurts, and now I have to wait that little bit longer.

I box the curry up for the freezer and opt for a slice of toast instead.

Peter enters the kitchen as I am loading pans into the dishwasher. He looks glorious in just his pyjama bottoms. He smells like limes from his shower gel, and I breathe him in.

'Can I help you with anything?' he asks, looking around the sparkling kitchen.

I giggle. 'No. And you have a knack for asking that just as I am finishing up.'

'Sorry, Jen-Jen – I don't mean to.'

I snuggle into his chest, and he squeezes me tight. All is right in the world again and my muscles relax, one by one, until all tension is gone.

'What have you been up to today, honey?' he asks, leaning over the counter to grab the bottle of beer I have opened for him. He pours it into a glass with a satisfying glug.

Usually, I cringe when he asks me this. My days are so unfulfilling that I have to exaggerate the joys of shopping for scented candles or changing the sheets. Not today, though.

'I found the old woman.' The words spill out of me. I've been dying to tell him for the last five hours.

His eyebrows crease together, and he shrugs. 'Who?'

'The old woman. From the night we moved in here. You know, the one on the road.'

His eyebrows squeeze together even more tightly. 'Holy shit! Where?'

'In our garden.' I go on to explain what happened this afternoon while Peter roars with laughter.

'Trust us to attract the local nutjob! Did she really run off with a towel?'

'Yes! She just vanished with it.' For the first time since my encounter with the woman, I am smiling. Peter has allowed me to see the funny side and it's pretty hilarious. We laugh together, his arm casually draped over my shoulders. 'Where do you think she lives?' I ask him.

'Dunno. Local madhouse by the sounds of it.'

'Peter!' I chastise, jabbing him in the arm. 'Don't be mean.'

'What? You've got to admit, she belongs in one. She shouldn't be roaming the streets.'

He's right, of course – again. I can only hope she's got somewhere safe to return to. I take solace in the fact she looked clean and cared for. *Someone* must be looking after her. At least for some of the time. I decide to forget it and focus on the here and now. Focus on Peter. I just hope that's the end of it.

CHAPTER SEVEN

The day after the old woman's visit, Peter treats me to lunch out as an apology for arriving home late the night before. I take my time choosing the perfect outfit and opt for a maxi dress. It's probably the most expensive piece of clothing I own and looks amazing with a pair of strappy wedges. It takes me three attempts with my eyeliner to draw symmetrical flicks at the corners of my eyes, and I apply a thick layer of mascara. I look feminine and I feel confident as I look at my reflection in the mirror. I check my lipstick before heading downstairs.

'Well, don't you look lovely,' Peter says, greeting me with a hug. He's already standing by the door, shoes on and keys in his hand. He hands me a jacket, but I decline; it's too hot out today.

'Just in case,' he says, placing it over my bare shoulders anyway.

I don't know where we're going, but I'm surprised when Peter takes me by the hand and heads down the road on foot. Surely there's nowhere in Thistlewood as fancy as Peter promised. I'm intrigued.

He leads me down a country lane and we head over a bridge that takes us over the canal. My ankles wobble as I navigate the pebbly path in my heels. I feel sweat dampen my armpits, but I don't take off my jacket after Peter persuaded me to wear it.

The more we walk, the more glum I feel. I have never walked this way, but I have a general idea of the direction we're headed. So, it comes as no surprise when we approach the Stag and Pheasant pub. My heart drops. I was expecting more than the dingy local boozer.

'Oh, cheer up a bit. You haven't even been in there yet,' Peter tells me. His tone is sharp, but he gives my hand a gentle, encouraging squeeze.

'I'm okay.' My voice is far more high-pitched than I intended, and I swallow my disappointment.

'Look, if you don't fancy it, we can just go home. You said we have that ham that needs eating ...'

'No, really, it's okay.' I pull him through the door and to my surprise, it's more than fine.

Overhead the wooden beams crisscross the ceilings, darkened by history and smoke from the hearth that sits in the centre of the room, currently unlit. The mismatched furniture is well-worn, but cosy and welcoming. Wooden tables are scattered around the room, polished by decades of elbows and glasses. It's dark and intimate in here. Soft light bathes the room, highlighting flecks of dust dancing in the sunlight that sneaks through the gap in the curtains. The atmosphere is soothing, yet a light hubbub welcomes us. The clink of glasses lures me in and the smell of cooking meat makes my mouth water.

I should have trusted Peter. I should always trust Peter – he's never wrong. I glance up at him and he's beaming down at me, his smugness overridden by delight at seeing me happy.

A young, pretty girl with bright red hair takes us to a table beside a wall of photos of the pub in years gone by. We give the waitress our drink order and she wanders off, tucking her pen behind her ear. Peter links his fingers between mine over the tabletop.

'You're looking particularly delicious this afternoon,' he tells me, his eyes sweeping across my cleavage.

'Thank you. You don't look so bad yourself.'

'What do you say, after this we grab a bottle of champagne from the shop and have a bubble bath?'

I giggle. 'Sounds a little ... naughty.'

'What can I say? You bring out the best in me.' I run my foot up his leg and throw him what I hope is a flirty glance. It has been so long since I've spent quality time with Peter and I'm ready to take full advantage.

'Not interrupting anything, are we?'

I look up to see Laura standing next to our table, clutching the hand of a gorgeous dark-haired man who keeps shifting from foot to foot, clearly impatient with Laura's choice to engage with us.

'Not at all!' I tell her. 'Peter, this is Laura. She lives in Thistlewood, too. Up by the school.' I widen my eyes at him, hoping he can remain civil. Peter hates being interrupted, but Laura and Harry are too posh for us to ignore them.

Peter stands up and greets the couple warmly. I beam at his friend-liness.

'Why don't you join us?' Peter asks them. As much as I'm pleased he's being friendly, I really hope Laura declines his offer. I just want Peter to myself tonight.

'Oh, we don't want to intrude,' says Laura. I plan to tell her we'll do it again another time, but my mouth betrays me.

'You won't be intruding; it'd be lovely to get to know you a bit better.' I press my lips together. Did I really just say that out loud?

Her husband, Harry, pulls up a table to join ours and we have lunch together while I inwardly curse my kind gesture. Though the more we chat, the more I feel like I was right to invite them to join us. It would be good to start forming some friendships in Thistlewood.

'What is it you do then, Peter?' Harry asks, the second after the waitress has familiarised herself with the new situation and taken our orders.

'Project management,' Peter says, turning his knife over and over on the table. He refuses to make eye contact with Harry. Is he feeling threatened? Harry is ridiculously good-looking, I'll give him that – but he knows it. I can sense his arrogance and it's an unattractive quality. I give Peter's leg a reassuring squeeze. Peter is a more rugged version of Harry, more handsome.

'Yeah? What kind of projects?'

'I'm in the transport industry, mate.' Vague as always. Peter hates talking about work. I think he spends so much time in the office, he just wants to put it aside on the weekends. Fair enough. I don't press him, and Harry seems to get the memo, too.

'Busy man, then,' he says. 'I know the feeling. I don't get to spend much time at home these days, do I, Laura?'

'No. I sometimes worry he's playing away.' Laura rubs his arm, her puppy-dog eyes not straying from his face for a second. 'Then I remember he's got a gold medal at home, why would he play with a runner-up?' There is so much chemistry between them that it's obvious her paranoid jab comes from a place of fun. I like that. I like to think Peter and I have the same level of trust.

I would hate for Peter to have to work away for weeks at a time, though, I cannot imagine how much that would hurt. Laura is an incredible woman. Then, I think about all the time Peter spends away.

He would have ample opportunity to meet someone else. *Once a cheat, always a cheat*, as Mum would say.

Laura turns to look at me. 'Seriously, though, I miss him terribly when he is away, but at least I've got my Elijah. He's wonderful company.'

'Elijah is your son?' I ask to remind myself. I think she's spoken about him before.

'That's right. See?' She flips open her purse and shows me a picture of a portly boy with the deepest brown eyes. He's eyeing the camera like he's hiding something. The poor child probably just wants to be left alone. Laura strikes me as the type of mother who'd take photos of her child a thousand times a day. 'He's growing into such a gentleman. Isn't that right, Harry?'

Harry's wince is so minor that I think I'm the only one to pick up on it. 'That's right. He's most definitely a mummy's boy.'

'Oh, please. There's nothing wrong with that. A son is supposed to love his mummy. We're like *that*.' Laura crosses her fingers to demonstrate her and Elijah's tight relationship.

A knot forms in my stomach. I can only hope to have that kind of relationship with my child one day. I release a sigh and Laura looks at me with a narrow gaze.

'Do you think you'll have children of your own soon, Jen?'

My cheeks flush and I look to Peter to see how he'll respond. I love hearing him talk about our future family. However, he doesn't even look at me and his cheeks pinken. 'We're undecided on that,' he says.

My heart drops and I force my mouth closed before someone notices me gawping. We're not *undecided*; we have talked about having a baby since just weeks after we met. Peter told me he wanted another child. Of course he wants a baby.

Laura presses her lips together. 'Well, you want to get a wriggle on. Wombs don't last forever, you know. I don't know where I'd be without Elijah in my life. Even with all the challenges he brings me.'

Tears sting the back of my eyes. I'm heartbroken. I feel like all of my pain is laid out on the table for everyone to witness. I feel sick. When the waitress places my chicken and mushroom pie on the table, I want to vomit right into it.

The meal takes forever, and after the dessert menu is brought to the table I am so relieved when Peter declares he couldn't eat another bite. We make our excuses and leave.

I'm quiet on the walk home, trying to focus on the sunshine and birdsong instead of the roar of betrayal in my head. *Undecided*. How could he say that?

Peter takes my hand in his and gives it a squeeze. He speaks softly. 'You know I just said that about the baby because I felt weird talking about that with total strangers, right? To me, it's almost like discussing our sex life.' He sounds so sad, so sincere. I feel all my doubts ease.

I'm an idiot.

'I know. I get it,' I mumble. And I really do. He'd only met Laura and Harry ten minutes before she'd asked that question. Why would he be comfortable talking about our future with them? Just because I want to scream our dreams to the world, it doesn't mean Peter has to. It's a personal matter to him.

'Sorry if I upset you,' he tells me. He gives me those puppy-dog eyes and I can't help but stop and wrap my arms around his neck.

'How about we get home and practice that baby-making?' I bite his bottom lip, a bold move for me, and he presses his body closer to mine, causing me to melt into him.

'You mean, have sex, Jen-Jen. *Baby-making* is a little ... cringe,' he whispers into my ear, his body tense against mine.

I nod up at him. He thinks my words were "cringe". I file that one away so I don't say it again.

We walk home in silence, Peter gripping my hand, practically pulling me along. There's an edge to him I haven't seen before and I don't know how to handle it, so I follow his lead and keep quiet.

The second we stumble through the door, Peter pulls me to him and kisses me while hitching up my dress, exposing my tiny underwear. Then, he pushes me hard against the wall before he digs his hands into my waist to scoop me up. I moan into his neck in both pleasure and pain. He carries me upstairs, kissing me, devouring me.

As we head across the landing towards our bedroom he stops mid-kiss, leaving my mouth groping for his. 'What's going on in there?' His face has turned white, and he lets go of me, letting me slide down to stand on the floor.

I follow his gaze. He's glaring straight at the third bedroom – the soon-to-be nursery – which I have spent a bit of time sprucing up this week. 'Oh, it's nothing, just some paint samples.' I tug him towards our bedroom, but he pulls back, stepping towards the nursery.

'Holy shit, Jen.'

His eyes are dancing around the room. I didn't want him to find out like this. I was going to surprise him with a big reveal once it was finished.

'Do you like it?' I ask him, my voice tinged with hope.

I have painted little bunnies around the skirting board – bouncing around, flipping over, being generally cute. It took me forever, but by the time I got to the last one, I had it nailed. I'm so proud of my artistic growth. I have also painted sunshine on one wall, and fluffy clouds and bright rainbows litter the other walls. It's beautiful, if I do say so myself.

'Do you like it?' I repeat. Peter's white face has turned a terrifying shade of maroon and I take a step away from him. He doesn't like it. 'I can change it if you like. I mean, if we have a boy, I can change it to dinosaurs. Or, football or something. If you think it's too girly ...'

'Jen,' he breathes. 'This is all just ... too much.'

'I can paint over the bunnies?'

'No, Jen. This, all this, is just way too much. This baby *obsession* is driving me mad.'

I gulp back a sob. 'I thought we were on the same page. I thought you wanted a baby? I might be a little eager, but preparation is important ...'

'For fuck's sake, Jen! It's like that's all you've got to talk about. Baby this, baby that! You're like a broken record.' He stomps over to the pale blue curtains. 'I can't fucking do this!' He rips the curtains down. I yelp and clutch at my chest.

'Peter, I'm so sorry, I didn't mean to upset you. You're right, this is all too much, too soon. I mean, we haven't even started trying yet. I'm being silly.' My tears are falling and every muscle in my body is vibrating.

Peter is standing in the middle of the room, clutching the curtains to his chest. 'No, Jen. I'm done with this bullshit. You need to make a decision. If you want a baby, you need to fuck off and find a man who is mug enough to give you one.' He gesticulates wildly around him. 'Or you can stay here and help me build something perfect. I want to provide everything for you, Jen-Jen. The whole world. You're not that ungrateful. I know you aren't.'

He visibly deflates in front of me. 'You were just so excited and I didn't know how to tell you before, but I don't want a baby, Jen-Jen. I just don't. Not now, not ever. I just want *you*.'

It's like my world has snapped in half. My hand immediately lands on my lower abdomen; it's as if my uterus has been ripped out and pulled apart. My mouth bobs open, but nothing comes out except a cry.

Frustrated by my lack of response, Peter groans, slams the curtains down onto the floor, and leaves the room. I crouch into the corner and sob, the smiling bunnies mocking me with their joy.

CHAPTER EIGHT

P eter didn't come to bed last night. After our fight he walked out, and by the time he came home I was tucked up in bed, my head pounding from my downpour of tears. He opted to sleep on the sofa, his snores drifting upstairs. He only snores when he drinks and judging by the number of cans left on the living room floor this morning, he must have been incredibly drunk.

I got up early to shower, ready to face him with a clearer head and an apology, but when I went downstairs at seven o'clock he was gone, and now he isn't answering his phone.

I feel sick.

I don't know what happened yesterday. Peter is under so much pressure at the minute with work and providing for me, it's no wonder he's got cold feet. I really think if I give him space, he will come round. This isn't over. I need to be patient. I just need to show him how perfect things could be, and he'll be ready to start a family with me.

At ten o'clock, I drive out to B&Q to grab a massive bucket of magnolia paint. The sooner I get rid of that silly room, the better. As soon as I get home, I don the my painting clothes and get to work.

My roller hovers over the glorious sunshine. I went to great lengths figuring out how to swirl in shades of yellow and orange to make it look warm and extra realistic. Then I had taken a YouTube masterclass on drawing cartoon rabbits. I was such a fool.

I splash paint on the wall, furiously destroying the evidence of my idiocy. Paint blobs onto my face and hair, but I don't care. My artwork reflects my pain and my arm flails wildly, desperate to remove my agony.

Tears drip off my nose and I wipe them with the back of my sleeve, smearing paint across my skin. I groan, loud and guttural, before throwing the roller onto the plastic sheet and chucking myself into a heap in the middle of the room. I tuck my knees to my chin and sob hysterically, my sorrow now too overwhelming to contain. Any hint of optimism I had felt before is long gone and replaced by misery.

I hear the doorbell ring, but choose to ignore it. Now is not the time to receive guests.

Seconds pass and my visitor presses the doorbell again, twice.

'Fuck's sake,' I mutter, before getting up to stomp down the stairs. I am fully prepared to tell whoever this is to get lost. How dare they interrupt my grief?

But, when I pull the door open I find myself saying, 'Hello? How can I help?' I curse my manners and my mother for instilling them in me.

'Oh my God, are you okay? You look like shit.'

I know I look awful. My face must be beetroot-red and my tears have mixed with snot and paint to make my skin a sticky mess. But, I'm still taken aback that this lady has mentioned it. It's very rude.

'I'm fine,' I tell her. The lie is so obvious, I can't help laughing. The laugh bubbles up from my belly and once it escapes, more just keep on coming. Then I'm a blur of emotions. My laughs come out as sobs and my tears still fall. I have no idea what is going on.

'Let's get you inside. I'll put the kettle on.' The kind lady ushers me inside and leads me straight into the kitchen and sits me on a stool. She sets down what appears to be a bag of laundry and grabs the kitchen paper off the worktop. She gives the whole roll to me before turning to flick the kettle on. She's so efficient; so impressive.

My sob-laughs finally subside as the lady stirs milk into my tea. I wipe my face and take deep breaths before I find the strength to speak.

'Thank you,' I say, taking the tea from her.

'It's no bother. Are you okay now?'

She looks at me through blue eyes, and her face is chubby and warm. She is wearing a stained Guns N' Roses T-shirt that she's tucked into dark skinny jeans. Her flip-flops have obviously seen better days and the nail polish on her toenails is severely chipped. Suddenly, my meltdown doesn't feel so silly – this woman clearly doesn't bother with appearances. I nod. We both know it's rubbish, but at least the crying has stopped. We slip into a comfortable silence while we sip our tea.

'Who are you?' I finally ask, peering over my cup.

'Good question!' she laughs. 'I can't believe I haven't introduced myself yet, and here I am helping myself to your kettle and tea.'

'Yeah, well, I don't think you expected to be greeted by someone mid-breakdown.'

'Oh, it's nothing. I've handled worse, trust me.' She holds her hand out to me. 'I'm Kay. I live next door.'

'Oh, hi! I have been meaning to introduce myself to you for weeks, I've just been so busy ...'

She waves my excuse away. 'Oh, don't you worry about that. I'm the queen of busy.'

'With the children?' I ask, the question stinging after last night's revelation.

'Yeah. They're good girls, don't get me wrong, but they like to keep me on my toes.' She takes another sip of tea. 'Though they've got nothing on Nana, as I'm sure you can appreciate.'

'Nana?'

'Yeah – the wacky lady who stole your towel yesterday!' She jerks her head at the carrier bag of laundry she set down on my counter, and I spy my blue towel poking out of the top, washed and fluffed from a tumble dryer.

I remember what Greg said to me about Kay having not two but three kids to care for, and it suddenly makes sense. She cares for the old woman, too! The realisation drops hard. 'She's your Nana!'

Kay laughs. 'She sure is. Sorry, I thought you knew she lived next to you. I came round to apologise for her escapades, and I've brought your towel back, washed and dried back to its former fluffy self.'

I am so taken aback by her revelation about Nana that I don't know what to say. She lives next door? This whole time, she's been right next door. Goosebumps erupt over every inch of my skin. This Nana lady escaped on one of the coldest nights of the year. She was eating my flowers. So, that means Kay isn't caring for her like she really needs. That surprises me, because despite Kay's appearance, she seems so efficient and no-nonsense.

It's like she reads my mind. 'Don't get me wrong – caring for Nana can be hard work at times. She's a slippery old bird, but she's good fun, too. She absolutely dotes on my girls, and the feeling is mutual.'

'Have you always looked after ...' I claw for her name.

'Oh, just call her Nana. Everyone does. Or, Mrs Gardner; but that would be weird for you, having not been taught by her.' She laughs at her little joke, but I don't get it.

'We moved in here to be with Nana when she started to struggle.' Kay glances downwards, anger flashing across her face. 'Initially, she was living in an old folks' home, but when I found bruises on her wrists, that was the end of that, as I'm sure you can imagine. Now I'm just doing my best, working two jobs, with two kids and very little energy. It has been a hard, long ride, but I think we're just about getting into a routine.' I nod along, sympathetically. After caring for Mum, I get it. She continues, 'Even with Erin's assistance, it doesn't help when other lovely neighbours like to dig their nasty claws in and try to ruin things for us. But, we get through it.'

Who is she talking about? Are people around here really nasty about a mentally impaired woman and her struggling carer? That's disgusting.

'Anyway, enough about me. Why were you so upset?' She takes my empty mug from me and rinses it before placing it in the dishwasher.

'Oh, it was nothing. Just being silly.'

'There's no such thing as silly. In my house every tear is wiped away with a hug. You don't have to tell me the details. I just need to know you're okay.'

Tears well up in my eyes at Kay's sweetness, but I shake off my troubles. I don't want to burden this wonderful woman. 'Tell me about your girls. Do you like being a mum?'

She raises her eyebrow at me, squinting at my silly question. I don't know what I'm expecting here. Do I want to hear how terrible it is having kids, so I can start to side with Peter's thinking? Or, do I want Kay to gush about how wonderful motherhood is, to prove to myself that I'm right?

'It's bloody hard work,' Kay says, treading carefully. 'Life-changing in so many ways – good and bad.'

'You wouldn't change it though, would you? You never regret having them?'

'Absolutely not. Having a child wakes up a side of you so fierce it sometimes frightens you. You love so deeply, protect so hard, and you cannot imagine living without that side of yourself. It would be like half of you has died.'

'I want a child,' I whisper. 'I want one so bad.' A tear slips down my cheek once again, and I brush it away.

'I'm guessing from the state of your face, that fella of yours has other ideas?'

I nod.

'Well, take it from me – you don't need a man to have a child. In fact, both dads to my girls are useless pieces of shit. I am far better off without them.'

I force a smile. Her strength is inspiring, but being a single mum just isn't the life for me. I need Peter to father my child, and Peter only. I couldn't live without him.

CHAPTER NINE

It has been three days since Peter dropped his bombshell and ripped away my dreams. To make matters worse, the loving connection between us is unravelling and I have had such a hard time trying to figure out a way to strengthen it again.

When Peter saw the redecorated nursery, painted a neutral shade of beige, he gave me a brisk nod and I caught a hint of a smile, but that was the only acknowledgement of our discussion on Saturday when he'd declared he'd changed his mind about having a baby.

I want to make things right with him, but the pain is clouding my judgement and I just don't know what to do. I have been extra attentive with meeting his needs: making sure the house is clean; cooking him tasty and complex meals; and ensuring his suits are dry-cleaned and returned to his wardrobe before he even notices they're gone. Now, I'm tired of the silent treatment.

'Good day at work, honey?' I ask as he walks through the door. He looks at me for the first time in days, his eyes soft. I smile at him, offering a truce. It's over. The whole argument is done. Peter doesn't want a baby and I love him, so I will support him in his decision. It's what a good wife does. And, ultimately, I don't want to lose him. I'm nothing without him.

'Started off a bit crappy. You're lucky you don't have to work.'

'What happened?'

'Oh, it's fine. Copped some attitude from a contractor, but I soon put him in his place.'

'I bet you did,' I giggle. I love how powerful he is at work compared to my snuggle-buddy at home. The icy atmosphere drops. There's a spring in my step and Peter practically bounces up the stairs to take a shower. The conversation is done. It is decided. No baby. Just each other, and I'm okay with that. I think.

At dinner, we pretend like nothing has happened and it's actually rather fun. Peter is incredibly grateful for the beef bourguignon I have spent the day cooking, and I know that's his sweet way of saying he's sorry.

'You're such a good wifey,' he tells me as he kisses the top of my head, before heading into the living room to catch up on the second half of the football.

Wifey. My stomach flips over. I *am* his wife. If I can't be a mother, the least I can do is be a good wife. Unsure how I feel about that, I pull a bottle of wine out of the fridge and pour myself a large glass to sip on while I clean up.

'Come here, beautiful.' Peter pulls me close when I join him on the sofa. I settle between his legs and rest the back of my head on his chest. I have missed this. He wraps his huge arms around me and nuzzles my neck.

'What have you been up to today, then? Besides making me that delicious meal?'

Usually, I tense up when he asks me that because I have embarrassingly little to tell him. Not today, though. 'Laura texted earlier to see if I want to go for a walk tomorrow.'

'Oh, that's nice,' he says, but I notice his lower jaw tense and he won't avert his eyes from the TV. Does he have a problem with Laura?

'Yeah, I thought it'd be nice to get out and see the local area. Plus, it'd be nice to make friends. It gets a bit lonely during the day.'

'Sorry to hear that, babe. I thought I was enough, but if you need a friend, I get it.'

'Oh, no – you are enough. Of course you are. It's just a walk; it's not like we're best friends or anything.' I laugh away my guilt and give him a kiss on the cheek. He still isn't looking at me. I daren't tell him Laura is introducing me to a friend of hers who's looking for a bookkeeper. It would only upset him if he thinks I'm looking for a job, and would put us back at square one after we've worked so hard to put the events of the weekend behind us.

We continue to watch TV in silence.

The news comes on and the reporter immediately launches into the top story. I watch in horror. As much as I am troubled by recent events in my own life, it could be worse. At least I'm not missing runner, Sheryl Coombes.

'She's probably run off with another man,' Peter scoffs.

I doubt that, though. I'm sure I read in the news last week that a dead body was dug up from a shallow grave just last week, in the neighbouring town of Boscombe. Is Sheryl destined for the same fate? I look at her smiling image on the screen and a dark feeling washes over me.

***

'Jen, darling. It's so good to see you. I was worried we'd upset you on Saturday?'

I'm confused as to what Laura is talking about, when the memory of the meal comes crashing back to me.

After Peter's revelation that we're *undecided* on having children, he practically threw money on the table and dragged me out of there, my eyes wet from threatening tears. It was an abrupt end to a lovely meal.

'No, not at all!' I reassure her.

'You rushed off so quickly, I thought something may have happened?' I'm not silly, I know she's digging for details; but I don't want to appear rude by brushing her off.

'Oh, we just had to get back for something.' The lie comes out so easily, I'm mortified. I hate lying.

She just smiles at me. She's wearing aviator Ray Bans that cover the majority of her pretty face and her hair is swept back into a neat French braid. Gold hoops dangle from her ears, drawing attention away from her pink, full lips. She looks like a movie star. I wish I was so well put-together.

We're standing on the corner of Henry Street, waiting for Laura's friend Gill to arrive. Laura has already filled me in on Gill's bookkeeping needs and I'm eager to make a good impression. Now that a baby isn't on the cards, I need something to keep me occupied more than ever. I need to keep my mind from drifting to the unclear blur of my future.

Thankfully, Laura changes the subject. 'Have you seen the news this morning?' she asks me, her face suddenly deadly serious. 'They found another dead body.'

'Another? Not the one they found in Boscombe?' I ask.

'No. This one was just a couple of miles away from here, near the fishing pools. That Sheryl Coombes, apparently. Found her in a burnt-out car.'

My face blanches. I had heard the police had found someone, but I had no idea it was so close to home. It's like the bodies are creeping closer.

This is the third body they have found in a ten-mile radius from here. The first was two months ago, when a dog walker threw a ball for her dog. When the little corgi brought it back, he dropped it at her feet along with a clump of flesh.

The next was dug up over in Boscombe. Six miles from here.

And now, Sheryl Coombes. Just twenty-two years old, from neighbouring village Milsby, found in a burnt-out car near where the old men like to fish on a Sunday morning.

I refocus on Laura who is still chatting away like it's a soap opera. 'Of course, the police claim the bodies are unrelated to each other, but if you ask me, they're just trying to limit panic. It all feels a little coincidental to me.'

I completely agree and nod. What horror have I moved into?

'Oh, don't worry. What are the chances it's a serial killer? Things like that just don't happen in Thistlewood. It's too quiet.'

Laura's blasé attitude makes my breakfast shift in my stomach. Shouldn't we be more cautious? I shake off my paranoia. She's probably right, but I make a mental note to keep a closer eye on the news.

'Here she is!' Laura smiles as a lady with bright red cropped hair rounds the corner. Gill is incredibly tall and walks nimbly on muscular, slim legs only a yoga instructor could possess. All thoughts of dead bodies leave me.

Laura greets Gill with a hug, but Gill doesn't reciprocate and Laura drops her arms. I give Gill a little wave and a hello.

'So, you're Jen?' Gill asks me.

'She most certainly is,' Laura chimes in. 'You two are going to get along like a house on fire.'

I feel myself flush under Gill's hard stare and I introduce myself with a handshake. Her grip makes me wince.

We set off walking and round the pretty row of cottages that were once the heart of the village, and head towards the canal. Laura and Gill chat away about the new railway development that is fighting to invade village land. I have read a little in the news, but I don't know enough about it to contribute to the conversation.

'You'll fight this with us when it comes to it, won't you Jen?' Gill asks me, her eyes aglow with passion. 'You won't let them build that atrocity.'

Her assumption throws me off. 'I don't see why not,' I say, wanting to give the right answer. I'm immediately nervous about what I have signed myself up for. I'll need to run it past Peter first, get his take on things.

'That's my girl. They can't just come here and cut the value of house prices in half. Not to mention the impact on wildlife,' Laura chirps. 'I can't stop thinking about all the little birds who will lose their homes when they chop all those trees down.'

'And they'll be knocking the community centre down,' Gill cuts in, her tone serious.

'Nooo, really? Oh my, what will you do?' Before Gill has a chance to respond, Laura turns to me to explain. 'Gill owns the community centre – it's where she teaches yoga and hosts a whole load of community events. She really pulls the community together.'

'Oh, they can't tear it down, that would be terrible,' I say.

Gill shakes her head grimly, unlatching the kissing gate that leads down to the canal. 'I'll fight it to the death,' she says. 'Actually, the community centre is what I want to talk to you about. How experienced are you with creating accounts from scratch?'

I press my lips together. The sensible thing to do here is to lie and tell her I can produce accounts; I *really* want the work. But, I opt for the truth. 'I've never finalised a set of accounts by myself. I don't want to find myself out of my depth, so I have always worked alongside a qualified accountant before filing to HMRC.'

'That's fine with me. I don't have anything complicated going on. My main problem is going through the paperwork and piecing it all together. I must confess, I have been lazy with my submissions and now HMRC are chasing me for five years worth of accounts. I've got a tight deadline.' She steps over a pile of sloppy mud. 'So, how do you feel about going through masses of receipts?'

I smile. My organisation skills are impeccable and the thought of rifling through and organising a box of paperwork really tickles me. 'I would love to help you!'

'That's settled, then. I'll drop it off to you. You're in the old Dutton place, right?'

I blush. I can't have Peter finding out about this, not now; not while things between us are so fragile. 'Actually, is it possible for me to work in the community centre? I just need a little corner and I can tidy up when you need the space.'

'Yeah, no problem. There's a little office you can take over if you like?'

'Perfect!' I gush.

Laura claps her hands joyfully. 'I knew you two would hit it off! Why don't we take this walk to the pub for a celebratory drink?' She tucks her arm into mine and for the first time in a long time, I feel like I have allies besides Peter.

However, fear gnaws at me. I am well aware that working for Gill might just be the final nail in the coffin for my relationship with Peter. He can't find out. He just can't.

***

Almost two hours later, one bottle of wine has turned into three and I am soon very aware that I cannot speak as coherently as I would like. But then, neither can my new friends, so I embrace it. It feels incredible to let go of myself for just a few hours. I'll deal with the consequences with Peter later.

'Alright, ladies?' I swivel around to find Greg standing behind the sofa I am curled up on. I haven't seen him since he and Erin brought around my little Buddah gift, and it takes me a second or two to place him.

'Greg, hi! Do you want to join us?' I ask him, pleased to add another friend to my expanding list.

Greg glances at Laura and smirks. 'No, I think I'll give it a miss. Can I buy you ladies a drink, though?'

'No,' Laura snaps. 'We're fine.'

'Suit yourself. Well, I hope you have a lovely evening. I just wanted to be neighbourly and offer a drink, but I'd better get back to my lovely wife. Nice seeing you again.' He wanders off, his hand stuffed into the back pocket of his jeans.

'Uhhh,' Laura groans. It sounds like she's on the verge of throwing up, all airs and graces gone. 'He's always sticking his nose in where it's not wanted.'

'Oh, really?' I'm genuinely surprised at Laura's reaction. I thought Greg was okay when he came round with a housewarming gift, but if the friendliest woman in the village doesn't like him, there must be red flags I haven't seen yet.

'Yeah, chill out Laura, you're so highly strung,' says Gill.

'That's not true,' Laura whines in reply.

Gill chuckles. 'You just don't like him because he drives around in that battered old van, bringing down the image of the village.'

By the flush on Laura's cheeks, I can see Gill has hit a nerve. I stifle a laugh. How are these two even friends?

Pushing Gill's remark aside, Laura continues. 'Doesn't it strike you as strange that they help out that woman?'

'No, not really. Crazy attracts crazy, right?' replies Gill.

'I think it's nice,' I say. And I mean it. Nana is obviously a handful and I'm sure Kay is grateful for all the help she can get.

'Hmm,' Laura semi-agrees. 'It's such a shame what happened to Nana. Did you know she was once a teacher at the school here? She was really good at it, too. She made quite the impression on all of her students. Mrs Gardner was legendary around here.'

'What happened to her?'

'Age, I guess,' Laura shrugs. 'It's a good job she was nice, too, or her actions over the last few years might not have been so forgivable.'

Gill downs the rest of her drink and we both lean forward.

'What did she do?' I ask.

Laura continues. 'Rumour has it she set fire to the school last year.'

I gasp. 'No!'

'Yeah, and she smashed the windows in the corner shop,' Gill adds.

'She doesn't look capable.'

'Never judge a book by its cover, Jen,' Laura says, waggling her finger and wisely shaking her head at her own cleverness.

'She wasn't arrested, though. Innocent until proven guilty, if you ask me,' Gill says with an obvious slurring of her words. I can't imagine Nana being dragged off in handcuffs. The thought of it makes me curiously sad.

It's been a long day and tiredness suddenly seems to sweep through the group.

'I need to get home,' I say. 'I'll see you both soon, yeah?'

'Oh, definitely,' says Laura. Gill nods and closes her eyes, sinking into her chair. I give it ten seconds and I bet she'll be snoring.

As I walk home I take deep breaths, praying I sober up before I walk through the door. I loop around the streets a few times to increase my chances. Although, when I reach my gorgeous home that I share with my even more gorgeous man, I am surprised to find the lights off. Peter isn't here.

I unlock the door and call out into the dark house. No response. My heart skips a beat. Where is he? Oliver winds his skinny frame around my ankles, meowing for some affection. I tickle him behind his ears before stepping over him. I head into the kitchen and flick on the light. My eyes are drawn to the fridge where a note has been stuck to the door with a magnet.

JEN, I'M STAYING AT A HOTEL. THANKS FOR DINNER. HOPE YOU HAD FUN.

What dinner? I didn't cook him anything. I assumed we could just order pizza when I got home. Is he mad at me for staying out? I dig my phone out of the bottom of my bag. Seven missed calls, all from Peter. I can hear the sarcasm ooze from his words, and I drop my head in shame. No wonder he doesn't want to have a baby with me. I can't even look after a fully grown man.

CHAPTER TEN

I wake up with a start and glance at the clock. 3:04 flashes back at me, fluorescent in the darkness. I roll over in an attempt to shake off my sense of unease. What startled me? I wrack my groggy mind to remember what had happened. There's a crawling sensation up my spine. Something is troubling me, but I can't put my finger on it. Plus, I can feel the beginning of a hangover churn in my stomach. I listen into the darkness, praying Peter woke me up, having changed his mind about staying at a hotel. But, only silence calls out to me.

Did I have a nightmare? Possibly. Alcohol tends to do that to me. It's probably the bad memories imprinted in my mind of my mum's drinking habits. Turning her over and hammering her back to stop her choking on her own sick is hardly the stuff dreams are made of. But, I can't remember having a nightmare, and normally they're so lucid. I run my hand through my damp hair and down my face. My skin is clammy, so with that and the lack of other evidence, I can only assume it was a nightmare that startled me.

I settle back down into my bed and trail my fingers over Peter's side. I miss him so much it hurts. My phone is tucked under my pillow, on loud, so that when he calls, I will wake up straight away. I already know the answer, but I check the screen anyway. No missed calls. No messages. Where is he? And who is he with? I push that thought away. He'll be tucked up in bed, probably missing me as much as I miss him.

Sleep is fitful for the rest of the night. My nerves are on fire. I just wish he'd get in touch. I just wish I could shrug off this foreboding feeling. I need to know we're okay.

At eight o'clock I tread downstairs, still in my PJs. My head is pounding, and I grope around the medicine box in the kitchen cupboard for paracetamol. Bingo. I dry-swallow two before the kettle has even had a chance to boil.

Making tea is hard work today. My muscles feel heavy, and just tipping the tea into my mouth feels like a colossal effort. I'm hungry and thirsty – I want greasy food and orange juice, but the second I decide to make breakfast I immediately feel nauseous. It's a nasty, vomity cycle.

Staring into the garden, I sip my tea slowly. There's a light breeze blowing the blossom off the apple tree in spiralling drifts. The lawn is a blanket of pale pink. It's a shame; I'll be sad when the pale pink petals on the tree are replaced by boring green leaves.

Then I spot it. Something white and fluffy sitting in the tree. Oliver? What is he doing up there? He's never been one to climb trees. Although, I shouldn't assume. It's not like I know what his hobbies are when he's on the prowl.

My mind flits back to Peter so I try calling him. Damn voicemail, again. I don't leave a message this time, though. There's nothing left to say, and I can't risk crying – I am far too dehydrated for that.

The shower is calling me, and I wash away the smell of wine and sweat. Then I change the sheets; I want Peter to come home to a perfect me and a perfect home. The house isn't particularly messy, but I run the hoover around anyway and wipe down the kitchen, just in case.

When I am drinking my second cup of tea and nibbling a croissant, I notice him. Oliver is still sitting in the tree. Silly boy. Surely he can't be stuck? The branch he's on isn't exactly high off the ground. I slip my feet into my crocs and head outside along the gravel path, fully expecting to hear Oliver calling out to me in panic. But, I'm only met with an ominous silence.

'You all right, my little man?' I ask him as I approach the tree. He doesn't respond with his cute little meow, and he doesn't even move. The sense of dread from last night returns like a punch to my stomach. I pick up my pace. 'You okay, boy?'

When I push the blossom apart to see more clearly, I stagger backwards and a silent scream erupts from my core. I swear I have been delivered to hell.

Oliver is hanging from a branch by his little red collar. His sweet, normally soft body is rigid. His back is to me so I can't see his face, but it is obvious he's dead.

My anguish feels so deep, so physical, and I begin to fall. I land on the fallen blossom with a hard thump and sob from the depths of my being. Oliver was my connection to my mum. The one thing I had from my former life; my constant. He was so sweet and gentle. He didn't deserve this.

My poor, poor boy. I *knew* putting a collar on him was a bad idea, but all the websites said to do it. I sob until my anguish ebbs and guilt for not helping him sooner fights its way to the front of my mind. I stand to release him from his deathtrap.

It's not until I touch him that I notice there's something else not right. Despite his body being hard, his skin doesn't move properly. It feels loose, almost *baggy*. I turn him to face me, when Oliver's intestines slide out of a slit in his abdomen, hitting the floor with a wet splatter.

Someone screams. The noise surrounds me at an incredible volume, and I cover my ears, desperately trying to shelter from the ear-splitting grief. Then, I notice my mouth is open, and the noise is coming from my own lungs.

I lean against the tree, conscious not to slide on Oliver's insides strewn on the ground. But, I nudge the branch, causing Oliver to slip from his noose and land on my foot, splattering blood up my leg. I step back in horror and my toe inadvertently digs into his exposed rib cage.

The vomit I have managed to retain all morning evacuates with full force.

This isn't happening. This just isn't happening.

I don't know what happened to my sweet, sweet boy, but I can be sure of this – this was no accident. I will not rest until I find out who did this to my darling. I spin around, desperately seeking answers.

The curtain twitches next door, and I think I know.

CHAPTER ELEVEN

I don't know when I came inside the house. I was vaguely aware of hands that hooked under my armpits, the soothing words, and a cup of tea placed in my hand.

My cries have subsided, and have been replaced with numbness. I stare at the floor, wondering why I was so bothered about the colour of the walls when I should have been putting more attention into my little family.

Peter hates me. My cat is dead.

'How you feeling now, my darling?' I glance up and find Greg's wife, Erin, sitting on the other sofa, clutching her own cup of tea. The look of concern on her face makes me want to cry again, but the tears won't come. They're locked inside the anger building inside of me. I breathe in deeply, riding the wave.

'You've had quite the shock!' Erin goes on. 'I have taken your little pussycat down from the tree and laid him on the patio. I thought you'd like to bury him; give him a proper send-off.'

I nod. That would be nice.

She adds, 'I've ... erm ... cleaned up outside, too.'

'Thank you for doing that. That's ... that's a big weight off my mind.' My voice sounds like it's rolling around in gravel.

'Oh, it's no bother, my love. I take it your lovely husband isn't around today?'

'No, he's ... away.'

'Oh? Well, when he gets back I'm sure he can dig a hole for you. I'd ask Greg, but he's busy today.'

I want to ask her what she did with Oliver's insides. Did she shove them back inside him? Did she put them in the wheelie bin? I feel sick at the thought and my question goes unasked. I squeeze my hand into a fist as Erin rabbits on about God knows what. My nails dig into my palm and I squeeze harder, determined to pierce my skin, fighting the urge to go round next door and scream. I have no proof it was Nana, and if I go round there in this state I might just give her a heart attack. No, I need to restrain myself and deal with this appropriately.

'Honey, release your hand.' Erin places her hand over mine, taking the seat next to me. She takes my drink out of my other hand and places it safely on the coffee table. I release my grip. 'Now, now. Hurting yourself isn't going to help you. You've had a shock, but hurting yourself isn't the answer.'

'But ... I can't ... I can't just sit here when *she's* next door. After she did this.'

'Who, darling?'

'That old woman. The woman who killed my cat.'

Nana. I can understand why Kay calls her that, but why does everyone else insist on calling her that, too? Like she's some sweet old lady straight out of a children's story. It's disgusting, truly disgusting.

'You think Nana did this?' Erin asks in surprise. 'But, she can't have. I've been with her all day while Kay took the kids to the caravan park.'

'Well, she must have done it last night, then,' I shrug. 'You've got to believe me – *she* did this. I just know it.'

'But, do you, my dear? Have you met Nana yet?'

I shrug again. My cheeks are warming up and I turn away.

'Jen, Nana is very frail. She's a struggling old lady. There's no way she could have done this. Her trouble-causing days are well and truly behind her.'

Oh, please. I've seen that woman zoom across my garden with my towel flailing over her head. I've also seen her survive a harsh British winter evening in just a nightdress. I'm not in the mood to argue, though, so I keep quiet. I'll find my evidence.

'Now, I'd better get back to Greg. He is very particular about his mealtimes and he'll be back soon. You're welcome to join us for tea?'

I shake my head and thank her for her help. I need some alone time; I need to think.

'Okay, it's no bother. I'm so sorry for your loss, my dear. This whole thing is truly dreadful. If you need *anything*, please come and see us straight away. You know where we are.'

A sad smile forces its way onto my face. Despite this Nana woman ruining my life, people around here are really nice.

Now, I just need my Peter back. We need to sort this out. I will give him whatever he wants if he just comes back to me. I need him here.

***

When the front door clicks shut a couple of hours later, a sigh pours out of me. *He's home*. Oh thank God.

Peter peers around the kitchen door, a sheepish look on his face. 'Oh, babe, I'm so sorry,' he says, his gaze not leaving the floor. 'I've been a big baby.'

I brush off the poor choice of words and go to him. I wrap my arms around his neck and relish the feeling of his arms squeezing my waist. We stand in silence, absorbing each other. I can't get enough of him. I want to absorb every inch of him into me.

He pulls away first and sniffs the air like a dog. 'Dinner smells amazing.' He twists around, looking around his feet. 'Where's little Oliver? I'm usually tripping over him by now.'

I force back the tears. Peter doesn't need to deal with me crying the second he comes home. He looks exhausted enough.

'He ... he ... died,' I eventually splutter.

'What?' he gasps, his eyes open wide. 'Jen-Jen, I'm so sorry! How on Earth did that happen? Was it his age, do you think?'

I shake my head. 'I guess it was an accident.' I lead Peter outside to where Erin has laid Oliver's little body. I don't tell him my suspicions. Telling him will go one of two ways: he'll either march straight round next door and give Nana a piece of his mind; or, he'll tell me I'm being silly. Neither option feels very appealing right now.

When Peter sees the state of Oliver, his skin blanches. 'Jen-Jen?' He looks at me, desperate for answers. He wasn't especially fond of Oliver, but they had an understanding. They both love me and they both live here, and with that in common they got along okay.

I can only shrug, no longer able to hold back the tears now falling over my cheeks. 'I don't know,' I whisper. 'I just found him, hanging from the tree.' I motion towards the apple tree and he turns to stare at it, running his hands through his hair, leaving it standing on end.

'Fuck me. Jen, I'm so sorry I wasn't here. How did the little guy manage that? I'll check the tree for sharp branches – that thing's a deathtrap. Maybe the whole thing should come down. What if Max tries to climb it?' He's rambling, wanting to fix everything, and I love him for that. And he's so right. We need to keep Max safe.

'We should call the police,' I tell him.

'What for?'

'*She* did this,' I say, motioning at Kay's house. 'That creepy old lady. She needs to be punished.'

'Oh, Jen-Jen. I know you're upset, but you can't just throw out accusations. You'll get nowhere without evidence and just think of the upset it would cause ...'

I cut him off. 'Fine. Will you help me bury him?' It's not fine – it's nowhere near fine – but he's frustratingly right. What can the police do? They certainly can't bring Oliver back.

'Of course! You get inside and put your feet up. I'll do it now.'

I nod but rather than rest, I go back into the kitchen to tend to dinner. I watch Peter search the shed and eventually reappear with a shovel. He heads to the back of the garden, hidden behind the apple tree. I'm pleased I can't see. I don't want to see the undertaker at work. Instead, I drop the blinds to distract myself while preparing the perfect welcome-home dinner.

The sense of relief I have with Peter home is palpable. I'll be safe again. I'll be whole.

***

After a quiet dinner of steak with homemade peppercorn sauce and hand-cut fries, Peter takes me outside to show me where Oliver lies, so I can say a few words. The mound of earth initially makes me sad, but when I stare out to the field beyond, it all feels so peaceful. His time here may have been short, but I am so grateful we got him out of that city centre tower block. He's had the time of his life here.

'Goodbye, boy,' I whisper, touching his grave. Peter kisses me on the top of my head before leading me inside, to bed, where I thank him for being my hero in the way I know best.

CHAPTER TWELVE

We spent the weekend in bliss. Feeling sorry for my loss, Peter took me away to a spa in Northamptonshire and we enjoyed a couple's massage and facials. I didn't manage to persuade Peter to have a manicure, but while I had mine done he arranged for a bunch of roses to be delivered to me. The nail technician said she'd never seen a bouquet of flowers so big.

The entire weekend was magical. I feel like I have my old Peter back. The one I had before the stress of moving in with me started eating away at him.

When Monday morning rolls around, I kiss Peter goodbye with a sense of remorseful excitement weighing heavy on my mind. Today is the day I start working for Gill. The day I officially go against Peter's wishes.

This morning, I am heading over to the community centre to see what Gill has in store for me. The clouds are thick so I opt to drive there and lo and behold, by the time I pull into the large gravel car park, big blobs of rain are hammering my windscreen and I brace myself before running over to the already open door.

I imagined the community centre would look like an old school hall, complete with the odour of sweaty socks. But, it's absolutely charming and beautifully quaint. There's a small seating area to the left of the foyer, and lining the walls are shelves containing a variety of books, comics, jigsaws, and games. Under the window sits a kitchenette with a kettle and miniature fridge. Pictures of the village litter the walls. It's a cosy spot for patrons to rest and children to play. The hall itself isn't particularly big, but a stage sits at the far end of the room, giving the room a sense of grandeur. Bunting criss-crosses the ceiling in various shades of pink and purple. It's clean, bright, and welcoming.

'Like it?' Gill asks, standing behind me.

I spin around and smile at her. 'It's beautiful!'

Gill grins. She's proud of the building, and so she should be. 'Good, glad you like it. Want to see your office? I have to warn you, it's not a pretty sight. You might do a runner.'

I scoff but, truthfully, I am a little nervous. What if this is way out of my depth? I have always had a qualified accountant to guide me and bounce ideas off; now I'm all alone, bearing all of the responsibility. Gill leads me into a little side room off the seating area. The office is tiny, barely more than a cupboard, but there is a small desk and Gill has set up her laptop for me to work on.

There's a box sitting on the only bit of floor space. I take a look inside, expecting to find handfuls of screwed-up receipts, but to my surprise there's only a small stack of papers. This doesn't look so bad.

Then, Gill bursts my bubble. 'Will you help me bring the others in? They're in my car.'

Ah, now that makes more sense.

As I'm leaving the building, my phone rings and when I see Peter's name on the screen I press the big red button, hanging up on him with a huge sense of guilt. I can't do this now. I can't lie to him when I'm smack-bang in the middle of the thing I'm lying about.

By the time we have finished carting the boxes into the building, we're both drenched through. We've lined the boxes along an entire wall in the seating area, two rows high.

'Actually, you may need to work in here. I think the office will be too small.'

I laugh. I don't mean to sound rude, but once the laughter escapes me, I can't stop. Gill watches me with a frown on her face. 'I'm sorry,' I gasp, forcing myself to calm down. 'There's just so *much*!'

My heart skips a beat as Gill's frown deepens and she presses her lips together. Have I overstepped? I can't work Gill out – she's so serious, so blunt. I wouldn't want to cross her. But, at the same time, her honesty is endearing. I wait to see how she responds, my mind unable to find the words to end this stalemate. Eventually, a smile cracks open on her face and a belly laugh rolls out of her, punctuated by sharp coughs, like she's using muscles that don't normally get a workout in her yoga sessions.

'I have somewhat *neglected* this job,' she admits. 'If I'm honest, I'm scared that if I don't get it sorted soon, HMRC will lose patience with me and throw me in prison. They're already threatening me with a massive fine.'

'I'd better get on with it, then,' I say, rubbing my hands together. Now that I'm here, I'm looking forward to getting stuck in. My hands are itching to dive into the boxes to sort through everything. I've got a sense of purpose again and it feels so good.

'You'll find all kinds of crap in these. Just put aside anything that looks personal and I'll go through it later. You'll find all kinds of receipts – catering for parties, bills, fees – all the normal expenses you'd expect for a place like this.'

'It looks like this is a popular venue!'

'Oh, yeah. We have people from all over the Midlands come here for their wedding receptions, team events, charity quizzes – all sorts. Plus, I put on yoga, pilates, and mediation workshops. I'm a busy woman.' She grins at me. I notice for the first time that her teeth are slightly crooked. Gill isn't married and doesn't have children, but she comes across so confident in her lone-wolf lifestyle. It's not a path I could choose, but it's admirable all the same.

As soon as I am elbow-deep in the first box of receipts, Gill makes her excuses and leaves me to it, giving me my own set of keys so I can work whenever I like. I just have to promise to stack and lock the boxes in the office before I leave. I work methodically, separating sales invoices from purchase receipts, each pile subdivided into tax years. I listen to Whitney Houston's Greatest Hits as I work and I'm soon lost in concentration.

Peter has called me another two times since I began and I can almost feel his annoyance with each vibration of my phone. I have never missed a call from him – especially on purpose. But, I really want this job and if he senses I'm lying to him, it's game over. For now, this will remain my little secret and once I have a little money in the bank, I can take Peter out for a lavish meal to tell him the truth. He's an ambitious man himself, I'm sure he'll understand.

Time slips away from me and when I finally glance at my watch, it's after five o'clock and panic rips through me. I haven't prepared dinner yet and Peter has promised to be home a little earlier tonight, providing traffic doesn't hold him up. I shove the boxes in the office and lock all the doors before racing home.

The lights are off when I get in and I breathe a sigh of relief. I've got a few pies in the freezer for emergencies, and I drag one out, praying it defrosts okay in a low-temperature oven. I go to stash the box in the kitchen bin, but it's full, so I grab the bag and take it to the wheelie bin down the side of the house. Dusk is settling in and there's an earthy scent in the air from the rain muddying the surrounding fields.

As I round the corner to the side path, I stop in horror and take a step back. Flies surround the bin, creating a blurry chaos and the air is heavy with the stench of rot. The scent sticks to the inside of my nose and shrouds my entire body. It's like something out of a Stephen King novel.

The flies are focused on the general waste bin, like they're clamouring to get inside. I lean the rubbish bag against the fence so I can retrieve the broom from the shed. It takes three attempts before I manage to hook the broom handle under the bin lid and flick it open. Most of the flies flee, but only for a second. They descend again in a cloud of buzzing black, immediately drawn back to whatever disgusting thing has climbed into my bin. I wave the broom to shoo them off again, long enough for me to be able to see inside.

Oh, no.

No, no, no.

Oliver's body is lying on top of the bin bags, his insides pooling around his sweet, little face. Maggots are weaving in and out of his eyes and mouth, devouring his flesh. I retch and dry heave, and clamp my hand over my mouth so I don't inhale the flies.

How did Oliver get here? Did Peter not bury him?

'Ah, jeez, caught red-handed,' Peter laughs from behind me, making me jump. I spin to look at him, my eyes wide. 'I knew I should have just thrown him over the fence and let the foxes get him.'

'You did this?' My words come out as a wheeze. The flies have continued their assault on the bin, relieved to finally have easy access to the prize.

'Come inside, let's get away from this mess. You can take the bin out later.' Peter holds his hand out to me, but I can't bring myself to take it. Still, I follow him inside, unable to stand by Oliver's rotting corpse any longer.

'What's for dinner? I'm starving.' Peter takes off his suit jacket and lays it over the kitchen side, no doubt for me to put away on his behalf. I can't believe he has the audacity to pretend like nothing's happened. I don't respond. I just stand here blinking at him. 'You all right, babe?'

'You put Oliver in the bin, Peter. Like a piece of rubbish.'

He sighs and frowns at me. 'Look, I started to dig a hole but it just seemed a bit ... gross, burying him in the garden. What if another animal dug him up?'

'So you put him in the bin? Like rubbish?'

'You need to understand, Jen, he's not your little cat anymore. He's just ... nothing. And in my defence, you weren't supposed to find out.'

'He's *nothing*?'

Peter nods like he's made a good point.

'When Mum died, was she *nothing*, too?'

'Oh, now you're just being silly. Your mum was a human. Oliver was just a cat.'

'*Just*,' I gasp, and turn away. I can't look at him right now. The image of Oliver's decomposing body is burned into the back of my eyes. He deserved more than this. That little guy was the best cat; he deserved the best burial. A sob erupts from my chest.

'Oh, come on now, Jen. Don't you think you're overreacting? You can be such a child sometimes.'

I've had enough. My grief fuels my courage and I take off up the stairs and into the bathroom, slamming the door shut behind me. I lock the door and allow myself to cry big, blubbering baby cries.

I knew Peter never really felt connected to Oliver, but how could he do something so nasty to him? *To me?!* I feel like the Peter I love is slipping away from me and I don't know who he is anymore. I miss him.

My emotions are bedlam, running riot through my entire body. I'm grieving Oliver and the old Peter in equal measure. I'm confused by this turn of events. Three months ago, everything was so clear. I was in love, I was living with the man of my dreams, my cat was alive and kicking, and I was on the cusp of trying to get pregnant.

And in the blink of an eye, it's all gone. My home has been tainted by death, my man is going off me, there's no baby in my future, and to top things off, there's a crazy woman next door hell-bent on driving me even more insane.

My self-pity morphs into anger. I have a right to direct *my* life. None of this is right and none of this is my fault. I'm sick of people taking advantage. I might not be able to get Oliver back, but I can have the rest of it. I *can* have my dream home, I *can* have my man, and I *will* have my baby.

I pull my contraceptive pills out of the cabinet and pop tonight's pill out of the blister pack. I hesitate for just a second before I drop it into the toilet and pull the flush. I watch the pill spin in the water before being sucked down the u-bend.

Chapter Thirteen

I didn't speak to Peter for more than two days after finding Oliver, and for days after that I could only grunt in his general direction. It was difficult to even look at him, knowing that once I caught his eye I would melt and forgiveness would be imminent. And I didn't want to forgive him. I didn't think he deserved it.

But, he's worked so hard on making it up to me and if I'm honest, I have enjoyed it. He's been coming home from work at a reasonable time every day; he's made me cups of tea in bed; he's bought me gifts. He even helped me tidy the kitchen after dinner last night. It's like the old Peter is back. So, the other day, I cautiously walked into his open arms and accepted his apologies for the pain he's caused. I need to keep him sweet, especially now that a baby is on the cards.

I try to push Oliver out of my mind, but even though the bin was emptied days ago, the wafting smell of his corpse still hits me when I walk outside. So, I have avoided the garden all week. I'm not sure I can ever go out there again. Between Oliver's murder and fake burial, the space feels cursed.

Today, I'm relieved that Friday has finally rolled around, as it means I have the whole weekend to focus all my efforts on Peter. Or, more specifically, on my plan to get pregnant with his baby. To get what I deserve.

It hasn't been difficult. One thing I can rely on is that no matter how late Peter gets back from work, no matter how tired and stressed he is, he's always willing to have sex with me. It's the only part of our relationship I can rely on at the minute, and it suits me just fine. According to my fertility app, I should be ovulating tonight. Operation baby-making commences.

Peter has decided to take the day off work so we can have a day together before Max gets here tomorrow afternoon. I appreciate his thoughtfulness and he wins extra brownie points when a local Michelin restaurant drops off a picnic basket.

'Peter!' I cry, closing the front door behind me with my foot and lugging the basket inside. 'What's this?'

He pops his head around the door with a boyish grin on his face. 'You like it?'

'Babe! Of course I do!' I have already lifted the lid and I'm admiring the crustless sandwiches, cream cakes, scones, and cups of cream with mixed berry compote. It's gorgeous.

'Get your gladrags on and I'll meet you outside,' Peter says, kissing me on the head and scooping up the basket.

I glance down at the summery dress I'm wearing. It's covered in daisies and skims over my thighs at a flattering length. 'I'll just grab a cardigan and I'll be out.'

He looks me up and down, his nose slightly scrunched up. 'Why don't you wear that long dress, the yellow one?'

I frown. I hate that dress. It makes my boobs feel massive and on the verge of popping out. 'I think I'll keep this one on. It's comfy. I'll grab the picnic blanket.'

Peter bites his lower lip and his eyes narrow. 'I think the yellow dress would be better.'

I don't want to risk my peak baby-making time, so I just agree and jog upstairs to change.

We head outside and stroll hand in hand over to the canal, crossing the bridge to the fields on the other side. We greet the sheep with a cheery hello, and they respond with ignorance and let us settle down in their field with our basket.

'I've missed this,' I tell him. We devoured our afternoon tea and are now settled back on the blanket to gaze at the clouds, my head resting on Peter's chest.

'Missed what, Jen-Jen?' Peter's hand grazes my arm, tickling me. A shiver escapes, making him chuckle.

'After what happened with Oliver ...'

'Oh, you're not still banging on about that? That was a mistake. Get over it.'

'No, no. I just miss spending quality time with you, that's all. You're out all the time ...' I feel Peter tense underneath me and I turn over to face him. 'Oh, I don't mean anything bad by that; I know you've been busy with work. There's no hard feelings there.'

To my relief, he relaxes and pushes my hair back behind my ears. 'You look incredible right now, really summery.'

I breathe a sigh of relief – I don't want to fall out with him. Not when things are finally slipping back to normal. Or a new version of normal, anyway.

'Thank you,' I smile at him and plant a kiss on his lips which he reciprocates with enthusiasm. Before I know it, he's pulled me on top of him and I'm straddling his groin. My dress has ridden up to my waist, and I can feel his hardness beneath me. I pull away – we need to calm this down and head home to bed – but Peter has other ideas and unzips his fly. 'Peter!'

'What? It's fine, no one can see.'

'Yeah, but, still, we can't do that here.'

He rolls me over, putting me on the blanket, his weight pinning me down. 'Peter, please. Let's go home and finish this off.'

'But, I love you, baby. I've missed this.'

'Then, let's go home ...' Missed *this*? I don't recall ever doing *this*.

'It's okay. Just lighten up.'

I open my legs a little wider and turn my face away from his. I squeeze my eyes shut so I can focus on us and not our public sur-roundings. He kisses my neck, his hands moving over my body, down-wards between my legs. When he pulls my knickers to the side, I gasp.

'Okay,' I whisper. I'm not ready for this. My body isn't ready for this. But, he's my husband, so I try to let go of my hang-ups and relax. But, when he pushes into me, I'm mortified.

***

I wipe away a tear, praying Peter doesn't notice I'm crying. He doesn't. He just gives my hand a little squeeze, grinning like the cat who got the cream. I don't know what just happened.

'That was exciting,' he says. 'Just what I needed.' He laughs like it was all a game.

I don't say anything. The strawberries I had at lunch are lingering in the back of my throat and I try in vain to swallow them back down. What just happened? The loudest part of me, the part that loves my husband and doesn't want to upset him, says I just had sex with him – al fresco. But, that tiny niggling voice keeps piping up – "I didn't want that".

Sex in public is so not me, and he knows that. We've talked about it before. It's so vulgar. But, I love him and I'm definitely sexually attracted to him. Of course he expected me to be okay with it; why would he think otherwise? I opened my legs to him. I've only got myself to blame.

By the time we reach home I am shaking with adrenaline, and I head straight upstairs to shower. Peter whistles as he steps into the living room to turn on whatever football match is showing on TV. The shower washes away all the shame. The hot water reconnects me to myself, ending my out-of-body experience.

I was being silly. My husband wanted to have sex with me, and didn't I want to have sex with him? I love him, of course I wanted to have sex with him. I just need to "lighten up". Besides, my prerogative is so much worse than his – I want to get pregnant without him knowing. So, who am I to say anything? Who am I to feel so sickened?

This might sound absurd, but I really think there might be a baby in there.

I hold onto that thought.

CHAPTER FOURTEEN

Where on Earth are my sandals? The brown strappy ones that go so well with my white skinny jeans. I need to get out of here before Sara arrives. Peter agreed that she would drop Max off and he would drop him back at hers. At the time, this seemed fair, but now I feel like I should have pushed Peter to collect him, too. I don't want Sara in my home. I just can't face her. I finally locate my sandals, squished between the bin and the wall, and thrust them onto my feet.

'You okay?' Peter asks. His hand brushes my waist and I force myself not to tense up against his touch.

'Yeah, fine. I'm just going for a walk, give you and Max some space.'

'Oh, you don't have to do that, Jen-Jen. Max likes you.' He bends down to place his glass in the dishwasher – something he didn't do before Oliver, which shows me he still feels bad. I appreciate that.

'We both know that's not true,' I say.

Peter freezes. 'Well, maybe if you stayed put and made an effort with him, he'd have the chance to get to know you better.'

'That still doesn't mean he'd like me, though.' It comes out before I realise I'm saying it. I know I sound like a petulant child, but I'm struggling to care right now. I just feel so down; so tired. Besides, whenever Max is here, Peter keeps him in his office playing that damn Xbox. They only notice I'm gone when the snack deliveries stop.

'With *that* attitude, I don't think I like you very much right now either,' Peter says. The doorbell rings and he leaves the room to answer the door with a snarl on his face.

I slip off my sandals, ready to face the music. As I walk into the hallway, the first thing I see is Sara kissing Peter on the cheek. His snarl is replaced with puppy-dog eyes. I cough to announce my presence and Peter immediately pulls back. He catches my eye and his cheeks redden under my glare.

'Jennifer, nice to see you again,' Sara calls over to me. She's far chirpier this time and her smile is far too big for a meeting with the ex. 'I was just saying hello to Peter.'

'Nice to see you, too,' I say, before turning to Max who's shifting uncomfortably in the doorway behind his mum. 'And you, Max, how are you?' He just shrugs, not even looking in my direction.

'He's shy, aren't you, boy?' Peter says, giving Max's shoulder a squeeze and pulling him into the house. 'We're going to have a great weekend. I've loaded that new game you wanted.'

With that, Max's face lights up. I've never seen him smile before and it brightens his entire face. He's a good-looking boy, just like his father. I want him to like me, I really do. He's the glue that can tie us together. If I can form a bond with Max, it'll show Peter how right we are together. Maybe then he'll stop pulling away and we can be a happy family.

'Can we play it now, Dad?' Max asks. Peter gives him a nod and Max goes to rush off, before turning to say goodbye to his mum. He gives her a quick hug before leaving us alone.

The three grown-ups stand around awkwardly. 'Can I get you a drink?' I ask Sara, wondering why she won't just leave.

'No, thank you, I best be off. I've got a date.'

'You what?' Peter bites. 'A date with who?'

'None of your business.'

'Of course it is. I have a right to know if you have a strange man around my son.'

Peter's hypocrisy rings around us. How can Peter have a go at Sara for seeing someone when the reason their marriage broke down was because he was seeing me? I turn my head, afraid Sara is going to drag me into the centre of the argument.

'Dad, it's not working, I think I broke it!' Max calls out from the other room.

Peter bites his lip before heading off with a huff. 'We'll talk about this later,' he tells her, thrusting his index finger at her.

Sara grins at me, her teeth a row of perfect white. 'I don't know how I put up with him for so long. I don't know how you're doing it, either. I was a child when he and I got together, but you're old enough to know better. And you don't have a child locking you in.'

My lips twitch downwards and my fingers automatically run across my stomach.

Sara's eyes widen at my gesture. 'Oh, honey, you're not, are you?'

'Not what?' I plead ignorance.

'Pregnant!'

'No.' I catch a sob before it can escape. 'I'm not.'

Sara tips her head to the side. 'Look, I'm not going to tell you what to do, but please just listen to me – you *must* be careful. If you're going to stay with him you need to keep him sweet, but at the same time, don't let him walk all over you. He'll beat you down and shape you into something you don't recognise anymore – someone you don't like.'

'I don't know what you mean.'

'By the look on your face, I think you do. I was with Peter for a very long time. I watched him turn from a kind-natured, shy boy, to an ambitious, controlling man. And, I'm no wallflower myself which, let's just say, drove him crazy.'

'Peter might be ambitious, but he's certainly not controlling.'

'You sure about that, Jennifer?'

Every event, every misdemeanour of the last few weeks runs through my mind. Sara is talking as if he's abusive, but it's a load of rubbish. Peter and I don't always see eye to eye, but that's only natural in a relationship, especially when that relationship has drawn so much closer recently. We're figuring things out. I haven't exactly been an angel, either. I painted the spare room without his knowledge; I took a job without saying anything; and there might be a child inside me that Peter hasn't agreed to.

'We're fine, thank you very much,' I snap. There's no way I am going to let Sara ruin this. She's the bitter ex, and I don't need her putting a spanner in the works.

Peter appears behind me, snaking his arm around my shoulder. 'I think you'd better go now, don't you?' he tells Sara.

'I'm off,' Sara chirps back, like she hasn't just needled her way into our relationship. 'Anyway, goodbye Jennifer, it was nice to see you again. And Peter? Like I was saying earlier, thank you for coming round last week. You were my hero.'

The second the door clicks behind her, I turn to face Peter, who already has his hands in the air. 'Don't look at me like that,' he says. 'She's clearly insane. She was all sweetness when she came in, purely to make you jealous, then she talked some shit about you needing to watch yourself. I heard her from the dining room. She's crazy, Jen-Jen. You're a clever girl, surely you can see that?'

I bite the inside of my lip. What he's saying feels right. Sara just blew so hot and cold, I don't know whether I feel burn or frostbite. Without waiting for a response, Peter gives my head a pat before heading back to Max and that damned games console.

I agree with him – Sara was acting really weird just now. But, I still don't know why Peter was at her house. I feel he's just brushed it off like it was nothing, but it certainly isn't nothing to me. I'm so confused. Why did Sara warn me about him? If he's so bad, why was he at hers? Is it even true? And if it is, why didn't Peter say anything to me about it?

My head is in complete chaos. Screw this.

I put my sandals back on, grab my bag, and head over to the community centre to work on Gill's accounts. If Peter can have secrets, so can I. He can heat up the lasagne later when they're hungry, I'm not going to do it. I'm heading across the green next to the duck pond when a man calls out.

'Where are you off to in such a hurry? You look very *determined*.'

I turn to find Greg and Erin on the other side of the road, unpacking their groceries. I wave and walk over to their drive where Greg greets me with a tight squeeze. He pauses mid-hug as we watch a police car drive past. Both officers inside are laughing raucously at something.

Greg eventually pulls away from me and I force myself to hide my distaste at the prolonged contact. 'Nice to see they're taking their job seriously,' he says.

'What are they doing here?'

'Ah, rumour has it they've discovered evidence linking the murdered girls to Thistlewood. Load of old tosh if you ask me. They should be arresting the bastards threatening to dig up our countryside.'

I see Erin is now laden with shopping bags, so I rush over to take a couple from her. 'Well, aren't you lovely,' Erin laughs, closing the boot door and leading the way into their home.

'She sure is!' Greg says, placing his bags on the kitchen floor.

I look around the space in awe. It's like stepping back in time. A huge range cooker dominates one side of the room, and antique dishes stand on a shelf above the stovetop. The surfaces are a weathered wood and the cupboards have signs of wear and tear, but are so charming I step deeper into the room. Every worktop and shelf is covered in quaint ornaments, knick-knacks, decorative jugs, and framed cross-stitch cottages. It's not to my taste, but I'm in love with it.

'Your home is gorgeous,' I tell them. 'I bet eating here feels like you're eating with ghosts of residents past.'

Greg bursts into laughter, clutching his toned stomach. 'You're right there, I hadn't thought of it like that. Ghosts lurk around every corner in this place.'

'Care to stop for a cup of tea? Or, I'm about to make Greg a sandwich if you'd like something to eat? I've got some fancy biscuits somewhere.' Erin starts to rummage in the bags by her feet.

'Oh, no, thank you. Another time, maybe. I've got to be somewhere.'

'You okay? You look incredibly pale, dear. Is it that cat business getting you down?'

'Leave the woman alone, Erin. She doesn't want you poking your nose in her business.'

I wave my hand at them. 'Thank you for asking, but I'm really okay. Maybe I'm coming down with something. I'd better get off.'

'Off to meet that Laura woman?' Greg suddenly barks at me, out of nowhere. He sounds offended and my back bristles. I'm not in the mood for confrontation.

'Why? Is there something you want to tell me about her?'

Erin is watching us both carefully, still bent over a shopping bag, but not moving an inch.

'No, no. She's just a little *fake*, that's all. You're a nice girl, I don't want you to get sucked into her lies.'

'That's enough, dear,' Erin murmurs.

'Oh, it's nothing to worry about. It's just that some people aren't what they first appear. But, you're a sensible lass. You'll see through it.'

Erin coughs. 'Well, it was lovely of you to carry those bags in for us. We won't keep you.'

Before I know what's happening, I am ushered out the door.

***

The entire time I spent at the community centre, I was a bag of nerves. I hate working behind Peter's back. But, when I arrive home three hours later, it's like I'd never left. I don't think Peter even noticed I was gone and I realise my stress was pointless. The lasagne I pre-prepared is still in the fridge, but I notice the snack basket I bought especially for Peter and Max is gone. I sigh and turn on the oven.

It would be nice to at least exist in the same space as Max. Even if he doesn't want to be my friend, then maybe we can share Peter a little bit more. He needs to get used to the idea that I'm with his dad now. I grab the bottle of lemonade out of the fridge and three glasses out of the cupboard, and grit my teeth. They can't stop me from going in there. It's my house, too.

When I step into the room, the smell overwhelms me. It's like grease, sweat, and mould all rolled into one giant ball of stench. They have closed the curtains and the game they're playing casts an eerie green glow over them, like the zombies they're destroying in their game.

'Who's winning?' I ask them with forced cheeriness.

Nothing. Not even a glance in my direction.

'I bet you are, Max. I bet your old dad can't keep up with you,' I laugh.

This time, Peter dares to briefly look at me before concentrating back on the game like it's an actual life-and-death situation. 'We're working as a team, actually,' he says.

'Oh, how lovely. Father and son working together.' I cringe at my forced joviality.

Peter grunts. Max snickers, which can only be a positive thing; at least he's acknowledging me now.

'I've brought you a drink. I thought you could use some hydration after working so hard.'

I set the glasses down and pour each of us a drink. They don't take them, so I wedge myself between them on the sofa and sip from my glass, enjoying the cold fizz hitting the back of my throat.

Peter shifts uncomfortably and there's a tension in the air. I'm well aware that my presence has caused it, but I also know Peter can help me shift it if he would just let me join in. I just want to be part of their team – not a key player, but maybe I can sit on the sub-bench or something. A happy bystander. I just can't be a nobody anymore.

I pipe up. 'So, what do you have to do, then? Just kill the zombies, or is there another goal you have to work towards?'

Peter huffs and hits the pause button. 'What's up, Jen? Why are you in here?'

'I thought I could join in – as a spectator or something.'

'For God's sake, Jen, can't I just get some time with my son? Don't you get enough of me all week?' I daren't tell him I don't really get to see much of him during the week, as he's always working. Even when he's at home, his mind is elsewhere.

'Of course I do. I just feel ... left out.'

Peter slams his controller onto the sofa next to him, making Max jump. 'Jen, you're behaving like a child. Go away! This is boy time. You get that, right?'

I nod and slowly stand. I pause in the hope that he realises I'm hurt and says something nice, something to soothe me, but he doesn't and I shuffle towards the door. On the way, I grab the snack basket off the floor, now full of empty packets. As I stand back up, my bum brushes the curtain open a crack, which spills light into the room. I quickly turn to close the curtain before Peter reprimands me, but his gasp forces me to stop and turn to him.

'Babe, you need to go and change.' His eyes are wide open and disgust lingers on his lips. Max has closed his eyes. My gaze follows Peter's to my crotch. Blood has blobbed through my white jeans, a deep-red mockery at my attempt to get pregnant. Humiliation rips through my core. I flee. Before I have even reached the stairs, I hear Max mocking me with an "ewww" and they both burst out laughing as the Xbox roars back to life.

Chapter Fifteen

I have spent the day mourning the loss of my potential pregnancy. It sounds silly – it's not like I have suffered a miscarriage (that would surely kill me) – but it feels like a huge loss all the same. My period might be light now, but it's also two weeks early. I feel as if my body is mocking me. I mope around, cleaning the house while Peter has taken Max to buy some new football boots before dropping him back at Sara's.

My mood is horrendous. I stomp around, enjoying the bang of each slamming cupboard door and the sensation of scrubbing every nook and cranny with exhausting vigour. By the time Peter gets home, I am spent. Too tired to argue, too pissed off for affection.

He strolls in with a smile on his face. 'Alright, babe?' I turn and plunge my hands into the soapy water in the kitchen sink. He comes up behind me, loops his arms around my waist, and rests his head on my shoulder. He smells like expensive perfume.

'Yeah, fine. Just cleaning the bits off the hob.' I hold up a little circle that sits on one of the gas burners.

'How about we head upstairs? I'll give you a good seeing to.'

I tense up. How can I sleep with a man who smells like his ex? I can only assume it was Sara. She's the only woman he's seen today.

'I can't, Peter, you know it's my time of the month.'

'Oh, come on, like that bothers me.' He turns me around and kisses me.

I press my wet hands on his chest and push him away. 'Maybe later, Peter. I've got a lot to do.'

He scans the room, taking in every sparkling surface (though I doubt he'd know the difference if it was filthy), and takes a step back. 'Fine, if that's how you feel about me.' His tone is sad, like a petulant child.

'I don't feel anything except busy.'

'Oh, please, I know when a woman is going off me. You don't love me anymore.'

My mouth gapes open. He's struck a chord. I absolutely fancy the pants off Peter; I love him so deeply it hurts. But, that's the problem. It hurts. Everything is utter agony right now. Peter is tearing me into pieces without even realising it and I'm scared that one day, soon, I will have had enough. I don't know how many more pieces I have left for him to play with. My silence speaks volumes and Peter nods at me before walking off, leaving me dripping water onto the floor.

Two hours pass and I have run out of things to clean, when Peter comes back downstairs. He stands at the living room door, looking sheepish. I put down my book and turn to him.

'So sorry, babe. I don't know what came over me earlier.'

I scan him over. Who is this man? He's morphing into a stranger in front of my eyes and it's terrifying. 'It's okay,' I say. 'We all have our off days.'

'You're right. You just seem to be having more and more lately. Is everything okay?'

I want to scream at him. Of course everything is *not* okay! My cat is dead, there's a lunatic next door, and the love of my life is scaring me. I don't know who I am anymore or what I'm supposed to be doing. I'm lost. I so desperately want to turn back time to six months ago when we were dreaming of our future together. Our dreams looked so different to this. We were supposed to walk off into the sunset together, hand in hand. Instead, it feels like I'm waltzing into the mouth of hell, alone.

'I'm just adjusting, that's all. Everything is so … *new*.'

'I get it,' he says. Does he, though? It feels like he doesn't get anything anymore. The only person he's aware of is himself. 'After your mum died, your world flipped upside down, right? And now that you've left that grotty flat, you must be feeling a bit … lost.'

I laugh. How can he hit the nail on the head, yet be so far off target? Yes, I miss my mum, but the truth is, I lost her so long ago that I've had time to mourn that loss. Alcohol took her away from me years before her death. And leaving that "grotty" flat was a relief – memories had leached into every surface of that place and it was suffocating.

Peter is right, though – I am lost. I have lost a part of me, the part that gave me strength when I had to take care of Mum. The part of me that knew I was capable. The part of me that knew I would be okay, even when I felt so alone.

I don't know who I am anymore. I've become reliant on Peter for absolutely everything. Money, happiness, company. It's gross. It's disappointing. There's so much I want to say to Peter, but I just can't find the words. I can't find the courage, so instead I just sigh and dip my head.

He kneels down in front of me, touches my chin, and gently tips my head up to face him. He kisses me gently. It's so tender, so sweet, it almost feels like the last few weeks of madness never happened. I melt a little, but I steel myself, determined to stay strong. He can't sweep this away with a kiss.

'Did you have a good time with Max?' I try to divert the attention off of me before I say something I shouldn't.

'Yeah, he's such a good kid. I don't know how he turned out so good with Sara as a mother.'

My muscles tense up. How can he be so mean about the mother of his child? I might not like Sara, but I absolutely respect her, and so should he. Plus, if this is Peter's way of distracting me from the fact that he's been secretly meeting with her, he's got another thing coming.

I open my mouth to challenge him, but once again the words fail to come out and I shut it again, shaking my head. What's the point? He's not exactly going to tell me the truth, anyway. I'll figure out what is going on with him and Sara on my own.

We opt to spend the evening curled up on the sofa watching a Marvel movie. I can't stand action films, but Peter has a penchant for anything with superheroes, and Thor is nice to look at so it seems like a sensible compromise. Before we settle in, I pop out for popcorn and Peter's favourite beer. I need Peter to be on my side. I need to draw him back to me.

He pulls me in close and strokes my arm and thighs for the duration of the film. He feels so warm and comfy, and it reminds me of where I belong: here, in his arms. He just needs to get the memo, too. We're made for each other. Or, at least I think we are. Shadows cast everywhere when it's gloomy.

My mind drifts to the baby I am still determined to have. After the initial bleed, my period has pretty much stopped, like it wasn't a real period at all. It was the universe's humiliating way of reminding me what's important to create a baby – a happy and loving relationship. So, I know I need to keep my eye on the prize.

When the film ends, I take Peter by the hand and lead him upstairs. His face is full of glee as he pulls off his T-shirt. I almost feel guilty for deceiving him, but I know it's the right thing to do. I know a baby is the solution to all of our problems. Our whole relationship has become such a mess. I know I can make him happy again. And, I suppose, deep down, I know Peter can make me happy again.

Peter pushes me onto the bed and flips me over so that I'm on top. That's when the music starts. It's plinky-plonky music. It reminds me of ... porn. Not that I have watched much, but sometimes Peter likes to put some on when we're getting intimate, just to add some spice. And I don't mind; I just look away.

Trying not to get too distracted, I kiss Peter's neck. He moans gently and pushes my head, encouraging me to continue south.

The music gets louder. Only this time, the sounds of deep groans join in.

Peter bursts out laughing. 'Is the woman next door watching *porn*?'

I lean up and look at the wall like it'll have answers. 'I guess so. Only, that "woman next door" is Nana. I saw Kay and the girls leave earlier and her car isn't back yet.'

'The crazy old bat is into porn?' Peter's laughter is so loud it almost muffles out the sound of groans coming through the walls. At least three voices are calling out, two men and one girl. All seem like they're having a great time. Peter looks at me and cocks his head. 'Don't look so serious, Jen-Jen, it's funny!'

'Is it? Peter, she's like, eighty!'

'And? Everyone has a sex drive, you know.' He pulls on my hair, not so subtly hinting for me to continue my journey to his crotch.

But, my mind is well and truly next door. I push him away and sit up. The groans suddenly become more desperate, like someone is getting hurt. The poor woman sounds scared – in pain.

'Peter, wait,' I tell him, tucking my knees up so I am out of his reach. 'This is too messed up.'

'Oh, really? I think it's a massive turn-on.'

'I don't. It sounds like that woman is being ...' I can't say the word "raped" after how close I came to ... nevermind. I need this. I need to go through with this. I *need* a baby inside me. I take a deep breath and lay back down on the bed beside Peter. I take him in my hands.

***

Two hours later, Peter starts to snore. He's been asleep for over an hour and the sounds from next door continue to rage through the wall, and now his snores join the cacophony. I give up and go downstairs. My hips are sore from Peter's overexcitement. I blush at the thought of my cries mingling with the sounds from next door, driving Peter wild.

In the kitchen, I pour myself a glass of water and sit at the counter, taking deep gulps, enjoying the cold on my raw throat. As soon as I'm done, I drink another, dribbling water down my chin. Eventually, I feel sick and slam the glass down.

Sex with Peter used to be fun and sensual. Now it's just ... angry. It's like he's punishing me for something. A sob escapes me. Then another. Each cry comes from the depths of my soul. I feel sorry for myself. Sorry for the woman I used to be: independent, strong, loving. And sorry for the woman I have become: pitiful, moronic, a pushover.

Why have I let this happen? *How* did this happen?

Suddenly, a movement catches my eye out the window and my cries abruptly stop. I stand up and step over to check the back door. The key is in the keyhole, the door firmly locked. I breathe a sigh of relief and head over to the window. Maybe it was just a bird that caught my eye. Or a cat. Not my poor Oliver, of course, but a neighbour's cat.

I peer out into the darkness, but my garden remains empty. The washing line shifts in the wind and the garden furniture sits untouched. Moonlight creeps into the yard, fighting to invade the shadows. I release my breath, clouding the glass with condensation. I relax my shoulders and turn to head back upstairs, but as I step into the hallway there's a tapping sound on the back door. Then, it sounds like a branch being dragged along the grass. Without even glancing back, I run to the safety of my bed and bury my head under the covers.

CHAPTER SIXTEEN

I have almost finished sorting through Gill's paperwork. Now, I just need to put it all into sensible spreadsheets so we can submit the figures to HMRC. It's been a hard slog for the last three weeks, especially as I have had to keep my visits to the community centre secret from Peter. It's not like he asks what I do with my time, I just don't like keeping things from him. My savings are starting to add up though, and it feels good to be building a little nest egg to spend on our baby when the time eventually comes.

'I'm off. See you tomorrow!' I call out to Gill as I make my leave. She's mopping the hall floor in preparation for her yoga class.

'Hang on a minute.' She jogs over, her thigh muscles popping under her shorts as she runs. Her physique is incredible.

'Everything all right?' I ask as she approaches me.

'Yeah, all good, I was just wondering what you did with the personal receipts you found. I just want to go through them, in case any are related to the centre.'

I point out the envelope I have left on the desk and smile, proud of my efficiency. Suddenly, before I even know it's happening, vomit works its way up my throat and I'm sick everywhere. Gill leaps back, but she's not quick enough, and my semi-digested lunch splatters all over her sparkling floor and up her bare legs.

'Oh my God!' I cry out. 'I'm so sorry!'

Without a word, Gill heads into the little kitchen and pulls out an old rag. She wipes down her legs while I fill a bucket with hot, soapy water. It doesn't take long to clear up the mess, but I'm wracked with shame, made only worse by Gill's ominous silence.

'Everything okay?' she asks kindly when we're done. 'That was quite ... spectacular.'

I turn away, unable to face Gill's concerned stare. I have never felt so ashamed in my life. Gill is an incredible woman to have remained so calm while covered in the contents of my stomach. Although, I bet she's used to it – apparently some of the parties they have here can get pretty wild.

'I must have eaten something dodgy,' I tell her, still not meeting her eyes.

She makes a non-committal "hmm" noise, not believing me for a second. I swallow down another wave of nausea.

'I'd better go. Thanks so much for ... *that*. Sorry again.'

She waves her hand at me. 'Nearest pharmacy is in Chilston, next town over. Or, the corner shop might sell what you may need. Next to the contraceptives, ironically.'

I finally meet her gaze, and I notice a twinkle dancing around her eyes. I bet mine look similar. I head off with a skip in my step to buy a pregnancy test.

***

Once home, I bound out of the car, clutching my brown paper bag to my chest. I am desperate to get inside.

'You look like you're up to something,' Kay calls over from her door. 'Like you've been up to no good!'

'Let's hope so!' I call back. A shiver runs down my spine when I spot Nana standing in their living room window, her arms straight by her side, her posture impossibly straight. She's watching me through bright blue eyes, a smile on her face.

I run inside before she can ruin my mood. As I rush to the toilet, I try to calculate when my last period was. I have been spotting for a little while now and I just put it down to stress, but what if it's something else. What if ...

Who knew three minutes could take so long? I squeeze my eyes shut for the entire time the test takes to process my fate, praying so hard. When the timer finally buzzes, I crack one eye open and peek at the little window.

I scream so loud. I scream for the good in my life. I scream goodbye to all the shit I have been dealt.

Two lines.

Two fucking lines.

I'm pregnant.

CHAPTER SEVENTEEN

*E*lated doesn't cover it. *Ecstatic* is too weak. *Blissful* is just the tip of the iceberg. There is no word to describe my state of being over the following week. It's a whole new level of happiness. Even Peter has noticed my change in mood and our relationship has become stronger because of it. So, now I wonder if I was the problem all along? Was I just too miserable and it was feeding him, forcing cracks in our relationship? It doesn't matter now. Nothing matters now. I've pushed aside all the blows that have knocked me down lately. They can't bother me anymore, now I'm pregnant.

I haven't told Peter yet. I'm worried that his determination not to have another child will dampen my joy, and I'm not ready to lose this state of perfection. Despite that, I have no doubt that Peter will see sense eventually. He's going to be an amazing daddy to this baby, but I know it'll take some persuasion to get him there. I'm not silly. But, the arguments can wait until I feel a bit stronger because right now, despite being beyond happy, I also feel like rubbish.

I am guessing the bleed that ruined my white jeans was an implantation bleed, which makes me four weeks pregnant, and the tiredness has well and truly kicked in. It's like I start every day having run a marathon overnight and it's affecting my level of care for Peter. He's yet to notice the reduction in meals made from scratch and the layer of dust on each surface, but it's only a matter of time before he does, and I need to tell him before that happens. And definitely before I start showing. But, right now, I touch my belly with peace in my heart. Everything is just perfect. My sesame seed-sized child can wait to meet her daddy.

Peter had a meeting in London this morning, so I haven't seen him since last night. The bed always feels cavernous when the other side is empty, but at least it means I could get into the community centre early before morning yoga started. I am so close to finishing Gill's tax returns now and I'll be sad when it's over. I need to start thinking about sourcing some more work, but that can wait. I want to focus on Gill's, so I can get this right. And I wouldn't be surprised if HMRC come back with loads of questions, so I need my focus to remain on Gill just a little while longer.

As I return home, Kay's door catches my eye. It's wide open. It's one o'clock in the afternoon so the kids should be at school and Kay's car isn't in the drive, so I assume she's at work. I hope Nana is okay. Or, has she gone out for a wander again?

I hesitate. I don't know what to do. I really don't want to get involved. All I want to do is pretend I haven't seen this and go soak in the bath. Heading down my path, I am unable to take my eyes off the open door and before I manage to locate my keys in my bag, my feet are stepping over the small fence that separates our front gardens.

My fingers brush against Kay's door as if they're nervous to knock too loudly. I take a deep breath and knock louder. The sound calls out down the hall. There's no answer.

'Hello?' I call out.

No answer. I contemplate whether I should just shut the door to secure the house and walk away, but there's a bigger part of me that needs to know Nana is in here. Especially as she's a cat-killer. I don't want her out there somewhere, terrorising another family pet. Nerves burrow themselves into my gut and I pat my tummy to reassure my little girl in there.

'I'm coming in!' I call out. I want to warn Nana of my presence – startling her feels like a bad idea.

Kay's house is a mirror image of ours, so I know the living room is the first door to the right. I poke my head around, but the room is empty. I'm surprised to notice that the space is immaculate. Toys sit in organised boxes in the alcoves of the fireplace, the carpet is pristine, and magazines lay splayed out stylishly along the coffee table. It's lovely!

Feeling bolder, I keep walking through the house to the dining room, then the kitchen. Again, everything is neat and tidy except for a couple of glasses sitting in the sink, ready to be washed.

There's no sign of Nana downstairs.

The stairs creak a little as I head up them. 'Nana?' I call out. 'It's Jen, from next door. The front door was open. I just wanted to check to see if you're okay.'

Silence calls back.

I walk over to what must be the girls' room. A bunk bed sits in the far corner by the window. Pompoms dangle from the ceiling, circling the entire room. Fairy lights wind around the top and bottom headboards. The walls are papered in a gorgeous pale pink wallpaper, and glittery stars are scattered across the surface. It's gorgeous and excitement tickles me. I can't wait to do something like this for my little one.

A strong smell of lavender draws me to the room next door, and I push the door open. It's like stepping into the 1960s. Vibrant colour insults my senses as I step over the threshold. Mint green and lilac stripes adorn the curtains and the matching bed sheets. The carpet is a classic brown-and-yellow in a startling diamond pattern. I step over to a chest of drawers on the far wall and peer at the photos in garish frames.

One captures my attention and I pick it up. A woman with long brown hair that reaches her bum grins back at me. She's sitting on a man's lap. His arms are tightly wrapped around her waist and he's looking at her with such pride and happiness. It's a beautiful picture, full of love and affection. There's no sign of the scattiness that Nana possesses now. In this picture, her head is clearly held together and the man, who I guess is Kay's grandfather, was quite possibly her glue.

Not so long ago, I'd have thought the same of Peter if he died. Now I'm not so sure. I push the morbid thought away. I can't think about that right now.

I hear a cough behind me. It sounds dry and crackly, like someone stepping on an autumn leaf. I turn to find Nana standing in the middle of the doorway, her hands clasped together in front of her in a prayer position. She's smiling sadly. 'That's Albert,' she says, gesturing at the photo I'm still holding.

'I'm so sorry for intruding. The door was open and I wanted to check that you were okay, and then I got distracted …'

She waves my excuses away. 'Albert was my husband,' she says. She steps into the room and I ridiculously take a step back from this tiny woman. She doesn't seem to notice and continues to pace towards me, wringing her hands together. She approaches the photo, takes it from me, and taps on her husband's face. 'He was a good man. You would have liked him.'

I nod, unsure what to say.

'You have a husband?' she asks me.

I nod again.

'Oh, that's nice, my duck. It's bad luck to have a child out of wedlock.'

I gulp. My mouth opens, but no words come out.

'I'm sorry to see your cat die.' The change of subject jolts me. 'He visited me sometimes. He was a soft cat. He liked it when I rubbed him behind the ears.' She stares wistfully out the window.

'Did you see who did it?'

'Did what, my dear?'

'Killed him,' I snap. I want her to just admit what she did. I need to see that she knows what she did was wrong. If she can't show any remorse then who knows what she's capable of, and I cannot feel safe in my own home. 'Nana, do you know who killed Oliver?'

She nods her head slowly, like a child who wants to lie, but is too scared to actually do it.

'And? Who was it?' I implore.

'Oh, well, that's a secret. I can't tell you that.'

I groan and roll my eyes to the ceiling in frustration. This woman is surely insane.

'But, dear, please be careful. Things are not as they seem in these parts. Everyone holds their secrets close to their chests, and some of them are downright dangerous.'

Is she threatening me? All of a sudden I feel incredibly vulnerable. I clutch my flat stomach, protecting my baby, and I step to the left to move closer to the door. Nana gently places the photo back on the shelf and turns to stare at me.

'Who's dangerous? What secrets?' I ask her.

'Now, a secret wouldn't be a secret if I were to tell you,' she says, and a grin spreads across her face as if she's made a hilarious joke. 'But, they're always closer than you think. You just need to open your eyes a little wider. You all do.'

I've had enough. I can see just fine. I can see the problem standing right in front of me. 'Right, well, I'd better go.' I head over to the top of the stairs.

'My dear?' she calls out. I turn back and find her just inches from my face. I jump backwards with fright, my foot catching the top of the stair. It grapples around for a solid surface, but only finds air, and I feel myself falling. I try to grab the rail, but my fingers brush the wood and I slip into oblivion.

CHAPTER EIGHTEEN

My meeting with Nana was eye-opening. I feel like half of my brain is screaming at me to be wary of Nana, she's dangerous; but the other half, my softer side, believes her. I don't think she did kill Oliver. If she did, I think she would have said so. I'm so confused.

One thing I know for sure, though – Nana has incredible strength. The way she yanked me back onto the top of the stairs is nothing short of impressive. I remained there, panting as I regained my composure. Nana just gave me a nod before wandering back to her bedroom, humming a jaunty tune. The last I saw of her was those piercing blue eyes that seemed to stare into my soul before the door clicked shut.

Her sickly lavender perfume sticks to the inside of my nose like glue. The almost-fall shook me to my core. I ran home crying, the shock and fear of losing my baby too big to handle. I feel too fragile to leave the house, as if a gust of wind could take my baby away. I can only sit in the living room, cushioned by the safety of my sofa and a good book, and it's where I have spent the last two weeks, eating everything in sight. Apparently, fear feeds my child's appetite.

'Honey, is that your third packet of those?' Peter asked me one night as I pulled open my third (or maybe fourth) packet of crisps. 'You should watch yourself, you don't want to get fat.'

I don't want to get fat? Or *he* doesn't want me to get fat? Thankfully, my tummy hasn't taken on the rounded pregnancy shape yet, but I am certainly looking more portly and I am blatantly growing an extra chin. If he can't love me with a bit of weight on my bones, then he can sod off. I'm just hoping that once I reveal my pregnancy, he'll understand. I just need to find the right time to pull the plaster off and expose the wound.

Peter has been to multiple late-night meetings lately. When he finally comes home, he's stressed and often locks himself in his office to work on reports and budgets, and whatever else he does. Allegedly, the project he's working on is proving delicate, but he's sure he'll figure it out. I hope he does. I hate seeing him this stressed and it's putting pressure on our relationship that means I can't tell him the truth yet. If I do it now, his current stress level might cloud his judgement and he won't see this as the great news it is. So, I continue to wait.

'What time are they arriving?' he asks me now, his hair wet from the shower.

'In an hour. You've got plenty of time.'

He pulls me closer. I can feel his excitement through the towel. 'Oh, yeah – plenty of time for what?'

'To get ready. While I finish this.' I pull away and continue to chop the vegetables, making it clear I haven't got time for those shenanigans. He tuts and heads back upstairs.

That's another problem with this pregnancy. I don't know whether it's the hormones, the change to my body, or the stress of the secret, but my sex drive has completely vanished. And Peter has noticed. At first, he brushed it off as me being moody, but I can feel his increasing frustration and it's only a matter of time before an argument erupts. But, in the meantime, I keep myself busy to excuse myself from having to do the deed. Besides, he's busy working. At least I hope so. The thought of him keeping busy with another woman niggles the back of my brain and I have to push the thoughts away to stay sane.

Tonight, Greg and Erin are coming over for dinner. They have been so kind to me, and I think it would be good for me and Peter to have another couple to be friends with. I originally asked Laura, but Harry is away this week and she didn't want to interrupt Elijah's routine.

It turns out Peter had less than an hour to get ready as forty-five minutes later, there's a hammering at the door. I enter the hallway, wiping my hands with a tea towel, to find Greg and Erin have already let themselves in. I smile through the shock of seeing them hovering in my hallway, and welcome them into the living room through a plethora of hellos and cheek kisses.

Erin speaks first. 'Sorry if we just barged in. Greg said it'd be okay, seeing as you expected us.'

'Oh, no, it's not a problem,' I lie. It's a good job Peter wasn't still wandering around in his towel. I stifle a smirk as I picture Erin's eyes popping out of her head.

I am bringing everyone a drink when Peter comes downstairs and takes the tray off me. He greets our guests with a confident warmth and Greg and Erin obviously immediately like him. I glow with pride. Here's the man I fell in love with.

'So, Peter, what is it you do with yourself? I don't think you've said.' Greg asks over our starter of roasted tomato soup. We're all sitting around the small dining table; it's a cosy affair and I shift to the left to avoid Greg's knee bumping into mine.

'Just project management. Nothing interesting.'

'Don't downplay your career, mate. You should be proud. What kind of projects are you managing?'

Peter shoots Greg a look only I catch. He's bored already. He wants his Friday night back and I can't blame him. He's worked over sixty hours this week and now I have put this on him. He's got the patience of a saint.

'It varies. But, nothing interesting.'

Greg opens his mouth, but Erin puts her hand on top of his. 'And I hear you and Gill are getting along?' she asks me.

Shit. Why didn't I think of this? Erin is going to inadvertently blow everything up for me.

'She's a friend, yes,' I say, hoping that will close the conversation. Peter is watching me out of the corner of his eye.

'You've been in and out of the community centre a few times,' Erin probes.

'I've been doing some private yoga classes. Actually, I think I'd better check the chicken, it's probably burning.'

I excuse myself to the kitchen, breathing deeply. Telling Peter about the bookkeeping work would *not* make good dinner party entertainment. I pray when I re-enter the dining room that the conversation has moved on.

Greg is mid-speech, waving his glass in the air emphatically. 'Oh, the community centre is the pinnacle of the village! It's the hub. Forget all the other damage the railway will cause. The loss of the community centre would be like losing the heart. I don't think the village could survive. The railway line just has to be stopped!'

'I hear what you're saying, but a link into London would be fantastic for the area. Everyone is fretting about the house values dropping, but actually, a link to the capital city would have the opposite effect. Thistlewood would be on the map!'

'But, you must understand – we don't *want* Thistlewood on the map. This is a quiet village and we like it that way.'

'No. Thistlewood is dull. It could do with a bit of life injected into it.'

'Sorry, lad, but you've been here all of five minutes. Who are you to decide what Thistlewood needs?'

'Peter, could you help me dish up dinner, please?' I cut into the disagreement in an attempt to lift the tension in the air. I knew the railway was a source of contempt in the village, that's obvious from the anti-railway posts and placards everywhere, but to hear Peter talk favourably of it is just embarrassing. I never knew he was in favour of it. Did he know about the plans when he bought the house? Did he buy here because he wanted to be close to the new proposed station? Does that mean he plans on spending more time in London?

'Well, that guy's a prick,' Peter mumbles into my ear once we're in the kitchen. 'Why did you invite him here?'

'I thought it'd be nice to have company. Unlike you, Peter, I get lonely here. With you gone all week, I have to find ways to meet people.'

'Yeah, well, in the future, can you do that when I'm not here, please? Besides, what about this Gill woman? It sounds like you're spending plenty of time with her.'

My mouth opens, but Peter's phone rings before I can find the words. He takes it out of his pocket, but whips it away again before I can get a proper glimpse of the screen. Although, I'm pretty sure it just said "S" calling. Is "S" Sara?

'It's Max,' he tells me, before leaving me alone to serve dinner.

'We might as well start,' I tell Greg and Erin. We've been staring at our chicken chasseur for the last five minutes and there's still no sign of

Peter. 'He's on the phone to his son. There must be a pressing matter to deal with.'

Greg frowns and Erin throws me a look of sympathy, so I tuck into my meal with pretend gusto when in fact my appetite has completely vanished. How can Peter be so damn rude?

'I take it your fella doesn't know you're working for Gill?' Erin whispers loudly across the table.

'What? How did you know about that?'

'Oh, Gill mentioned it in passing. Don't worry though, our lips are sealed.' Erin mimes zipping her lips closed, brushing sauce across her chin.

'Yeah, we don't want to upset him,' Greg says, condescension dripping from his voice. Something tells me Greg and Peter will never be friends.

'Thank you,' I mutter. 'Peter is just a little old fashioned when it comes to a woman's place in the home, but I get a bit bored sometimes.'

Erin touches my hand. 'I get it. I'm here to support Greg in the home and thankfully I have never had to work a day in my life, but we're all different, my love. You do what you've got to do.'

'Doing shady Gill's accounts must be interesting?' Greg asks me. 'I bet she's gutted she's got to declare all that fundraising money to HMRC. There's nothing worse than giving a wedge of your hard-earned money to the tax man.'

'Fundraising?'

'Yeah, Gill has no shame in asking us to dig deep into our pockets to raise money for the place.'

'When did she last do this?'

'Christmas, before all this HMRC nonsense distracted her.'

Red flags are flying in my head. The community centre is not a charity, it's a business. I've accounted for every penny that has hit the community centre's bank account, but I have never seen large sums received from fundraising events paid into the accounts. Where did that money go?

My cheeks redden. Has Gill lied to me or is it a genuine oversight? Dread weighs heavy in my heart. This is going to be an embarrassing conversation.

Why is nothing ever easy?

CHAPTER NINETEEN

Peter missed most of dinner last night. He reappeared during dessert and made a poor excuse about Max having a hard time at school, before sitting in a bad mood for the remainder of the meal. It's no surprise Greg and Erin made their excuses to leave as soon as the last profiterole had been devoured. I cleaned the kitchen after they'd gone, furiously scrubbing away my anger at Peter's crappy attitude and my annoyance that I didn't have the courage to say anything to him about it.

This morning, I roll out of bed hours after my alarm went off. I didn't intend to fall back asleep, but it's like my body is just refusing to function. I ache all over and my head is pounding. I am ravenous and head towards the kitchen to inspect the contents of the fridge. Peter has had to go into the office today. If it's the truth, then I do feel sorry for him having to work on a Saturday, but he says work will ease up soon and I just need to be patient.

Of course, he could be with this "S" person.

Whatever. I need some space from him. He can do what he bloody likes.

I enter the kitchen and face the horrendous mess Peter has left. It seems he's attempted to make his own lunch, which I'm guessing is some sort of apology. Usually, I make it and he brings it home again after eating out instead. His "apology" is meaningless, though, as he's left crumbs scattered all over the kitchen side, and a dirty knife still dug into the butter (which he hasn't bothered to put the lid on). And, there's a yellow stain smeared across the side which I'm guessing is mustard so is going to be a pain to wash off.

I sigh. How can that man be so selfish? I feel like the more time I spend with him, the more insensitive he gets. Or, am I just noticing it more? Has he always been this way and now my rose-tinted glasses are coming off? The biggest and most terrifying question I have to ask myself now, is can I put the rose-tinted glasses back on? Or, can Peter change his ways? I fear it'll have to be the former, and I'm not sure I have the attention span right now to be worrying about spectacles.

I turn away from the mess and pull the leftover profiteroles out of the fridge. I don't even bother to put them in a bowl, opting to scoop them straight out of the serving dish. I groan through a mouthful of pastry. Since when did chocolate and cream taste so good together? The baby must really enjoy it, so I scoop up some more, not giving a damn how disgusting I look right now.

It's only when there's a tap on the door that I stop stuffing my face. The profiteroles are all gone and I have moved onto cutting thick slices of cheddar. I panic and shove the cheese back in the fridge like whoever is there can see me through the walls.

I swing the door open. 'Kay!' I say. 'How nice to see you.'

She looks me up and down. 'Everything all right?'

I look down and cringe when I remember I'm still in my Tweety Pie nightdress and slippers. It's almost midday. 'Oh, yeah, just having a lazy day, you know?'

She smiles. 'I know *of* them. Can't say I get to enjoy them much in that madhouse.' Is she referring to Nana, the kids, or her overall busy life? 'You've got a little something just here.' She motions to her cheek bone.

I touch my cheek, smearing something soft along my finger. Cream. I lick my finger then rub my face with my hands, removing the evidence of my binge.

'Would you like to come in?' I ask Kay, praying she declines. I don't want her to see the state of my kitchen.

I breathe a sigh of relief when she shakes her head. 'I can't. Thanks, though. I've got the girls in the house with some sort of sickness bug, but I just wanted to check you were okay.'

'Yes, why wouldn't I be?'

Kay presses her lips together like she's nervous to go on. What's happening here? Why would Kay think there is something wrong with me? And why is she so afraid to reveal her reason? She chooses not to say anything and just motions at me to step outside.

I cry out in horror. Thick red paint coats the brick on the front of the house, screaming undeserved profanities.

FUCK THE RAILWAY. FUCK YOU.

The paint has dripped down underneath each letter, making it look like the words have been etched into the skin of my home. The letters are oozing blood. Who would do such a thing? And why?

'Any idea who did this?' Kay gives a voice to my questions.

'No idea!' I say through my fingers, my hand clasped over my mouth. 'Why us?'

'It might not be just you ...' Kay says reasonably. 'People around here are pretty angry about the railway. Maybe they went on some sort of rampage, and you were just one of the victims.'

Kay speaks sense. I'll go for a walk later and see what else I can uncover. Something tells me my efforts will be futile, though. This feels personal somehow. This was directed specifically at us.

'Need help getting it off? I can get Nana to watch the girls ...'

'No!' I bite too quickly. I can't be the person responsible for Kay leaving her children in Nana's care. I would never forgive myself if something happened to them. 'This needs a professional cleaner. I'll call around.'

Kay nods in agreement and squeezes my shoulder reassuringly. 'Let me know if you need anything, yeah? Some people really need to get a life.'

I watch her head back into her house, making sure her door is firmly shut before I let the tears spill down my cheeks. The net curtain in Kay's living room twitches and I see Nana's eyes staring at me through the glass, her face not revealing an ounce of emotion.

***

I spend some time contemplating my next move. Deep down, I know I should call the police, but they could take days to look at it, only to then tell me there's nothing they can do. And, keeping it there for the entire neighbourhood to see is humiliating.

Instead, I find a professional cleaning company who can come at short notice at a premium price. By three o'clock, I'm standing inside cupping a decaf tea, trying to avoid the fumes from whatever chemical the man is pouring over my brickwork.

When did the culprit do this? My first thought was it must have been done last night, but then Peter would have seen it when he left for work this morning. His car was parked in the drive, facing the house, so there's no way he could have missed it.

I text him to make sure. I need to know when this happened. If that paint wasn't there when Peter left for work this morning, it means this happened in broad daylight while I was sleeping. I feel violated. The thought of having someone wandering around my property, defacing its beauty, puts my teeth on edge. The attack may not have been directed explicitly at me, but my safety still feels compromised.

It has been an hour since I texted Peter, and he still hasn't read it. I know it's unreasonable of me, but I feel really annoyed at him. I feel like he doesn't care enough to text back, despite me being frightened.

By the time Peter comes home, it's getting dark and the remains of the paint are hard to see. The cleaner gave it a good go, but he couldn't remove it all and the first FUCK stands prominently in the dusk – a rather unpleasant greeting. I watch as Peter pulls in and he's glaring at the profanity before he's even cut the engine. It confirms my suspicions; there's no way he would have missed it when he left this morning. This happened during the day. Does that mean someone saw something?

'Jen!' Peter calls when he comes through the door. He sounds mad, like it's my fault. I stomp into the hallway – there's no way I am getting the blame for this. 'What's that out there?' He barks at me, throwing his hand out, gesturing outside.

'How am I supposed to know?' I reply defiantly.

'Well, why haven't you cleaned it off?'

My mouth flies open, my eyes wide. 'I *did* get it cleaned off! *That* won't come off with a dab of a sponge, you know! I had to call in a professional.'

'Well, they did a shit job.' He slips off his shoes and drops them next to the shoe cupboard, where I ignore them. 'You better not be paying them for that mess.'

'He did a great job, considering how bad it was.'

'It's still there, Jen!' He's speaking to me like I am eight years old, and I see red.

'Some of it is, Peter. *Some* of it. You want to know what it said before the kind man cleaned it off for us?'

Peter squints at me, daring me to keep having a go at him. I tell him the full insult, his eyes widening with each word. 'So, how about you tell me what project you're currently managing, Peter. Because I don't think you've been telling the whole truth, have you?'

He swallows and has the decency to look embarrassed. Guilty. 'Fine,' he says, sitting on the sofa and crossing his legs. 'Jen, the new project I'm working on ... It's the railway that cuts through Thistlewood.'

My shoulders sag. 'Why didn't you tell me that?'

'Because you'd blab to your new little friends, and you've seen what will happen if word gets out.'

I glance outside, expecting to see pitchforks marching towards the house. 'But, it's not like it's your fault. You're just doing your job.'

'Like they care. All they give a damn about is the village staying in the 1800s and if they see my name stamped all over it, they'll do anything to take me down.' Silence drifts between us as we contemplate the revelations that have just fallen out of his mouth. Peter breaks the silence with a groan. 'I mean, people were going to find out eventually. I just thought I'd have a bit longer to get things going before it all kicks off. And when they find out ...'

'What was your plan? Hide away until it was too late for anyone to fight you?'

He shrugs. 'I guess so. Why would I deliberately make life hard for myself? Anyway, the clever ones around here know how it is already. They're buying up properties, ready to rent them out at high prices to those who want an idyllic setting that's commutable to London.'

'And the not-so-clever ones?'

'Tough shit. We're doing it anyway. I just need to push them out of the way. Like the owners of this house, the Duttons. The silly idiots panicked and sold at a ridiculously low price. They let fear win and couldn't see the potential. And we lucked out.' He beams at me, proud of himself.

'What are you talking about now?'

'Think about it. Better rail links to London mean more job opportunities. This will drive up the demand for houses here and people will be making a killing. We've struck gold by buying this place!'

I feel sick. My sweet, thoughtful husband has officially gone. He's morphed into this disgusting, selfish coward full of secrets and lies and I hate every ounce of his being right now. 'You can't do this.'

'Too late, babe. It's happening, whether you like it or not.'

His words resonate far too deeply for my own comfort. It's how I am starting to feel about our entire relationship.

CHAPTER TWENTY

P eter's revelation has sent shockwaves through me. It isn't just the fact he's tearing out the heart of the village; it's also his ability to lie to me. I have been with the man for over a year. I laid myself bare for him, followed his dreams and made them my own, yet I had no idea what he gets up to all day, every day. I had no idea he could be so callous, so cold. How can he not care about tearing up miles of countryside and creating the financial ruin of hundreds of people whose houses are now sitting in negative equity, not to mention the stress and anger he is causing? I had no idea my gorgeous, kind man is so cruel.

As much as the state of the village is concerning me, I have bigger worries. I cannot stop thinking about how Peter will react when he finds out I'm pregnant. Ever since the incident with the graffiti, we've barely spoken. I'm starting to worry my bump will soon start to show, pushing us even further apart. My twelve-week scan is just two weeks away and I really want Peter to be there. I need him to see our little baby on the screen so he can feel the surge of love I have had the pleasure of feeling for the last ten weeks. I have no doubt it's all the convincing he needs.

I also can't help thinking that something might be wrong with the baby, and as much as I hate him right now, I will need his hand to hold. He needs to be there. If there is something wrong, it would smash me into pieces and if he's not there to put me back together, I will never recover. Despite how mad I am at him for potentially ruining everything we have here in Thistlewood.

My time is running out and I need to tell him the truth. I am terrified about how he's going to react. The whole scenario feels ridiculous. I shouldn't feel this way about my partner, the man I love. I should be able to go to him with anything, and three months ago I could have. But now? My entire world has flipped upside down and it's too heavy for me to flip back around. Still, I have a deadline, and I need to figure things out sharpish.

It's Saturday and the glorious August sunshine is beating down, so I decide to sit outside for a dose of vitamin D. With Peter now working seven days a week, I feel very much alone. It hasn't helped that now I know Peter's secrets – along with someone else in the village – I can't face anyone. I'm afraid his involvement in the destruction of the village is written all over my face and after the graffiti, I am scared of how people will react.

I'm lonely, it's true; but then I remind myself that I'm never alone. I rub sunscreen on my bare tummy, sun rays beating down on me, warming me to the bones. For the first time in a long time, I allow myself to relax, and my God it feels good.

Then the humming starts. A jaunty tune, sung with a husky voice. Nana.

I contemplate running inside, but why should she ruin my fun? There's a six-foot fence between us and after Nana decided to snack on my flower bed, Peter upgraded the bolt on our gate, so I'm secure here. I won't let Nana scare me away. How silly.

I close my eyes and lie back.

The humming stops.

Then it returns. Louder. Closer.

I peer over my sunglasses and look around. Nana is staring at me, her head stock-still over the fence that separates our gardens. The fence that was supposed to provide me with privacy. She doesn't move an inch, even when I jump up and back away.

'Nana ...' I finally gasp. 'You can't scare me like that, it's not nice.'

She continues to stare, only now a smile plays on her lips. 'You look very pretty, my dear. *Glowing.*'

I automatically cover my stomach with my arms and wish I was wearing more than a bikini top and shorts.

'Nana!' Kay's voice floats over from her house. 'What are you doing up there, you silly sod? Get down!'

I consider running away before Kay has a chance to see me, but Nana speaks too soon. 'I'm just talking to my friend here. She's a lovely girl. She was in my bedroom.'

I wince. There's a scrabbling sound from behind the fence and Nana disappears, quickly replaced by Kay's head popping up. Why can't they leave me alone? 'I wasn't snooping,' I stutter. 'When Nana found me in her room.'

'Oh, I know about that already, I've had a chat with her. Don't worry about it.' She waves her arm, brushing away my concerns. 'She's the silly sod who left the door open. I'm just glad you were kind enough to look out for her.'

She's right. I *was* kind enough to look after her, after what she's done. I'm also stunned that Nana and Kay cleared up the situation. Why is Nana lucid one minute and absolute bananas the next?

I'm in a world of my own, thinking about my interactions with Nana, when Kay's cough snaps me back to the present. I turn to look at her and I'm horrified to see she is staring right at my exposed stomach. I'm not showing much – actually, if I'm honest, I'm barely showing at all – but these tiny shorts really highlight my bump. Kay is waiting for me to talk, expectation and delight on her face. I know she doesn't want to be the first to speak, in case she's misread the situation. If circumstances were different and this wasn't a big secret, I would burst out laughing.

Instead, I blurt out, 'Please don't tell Peter.'

Her joy morphs into shock. 'Oh, no!' She has a pained expression on her face. 'Don't tell me you've been playing away.'

'No! Not at all. It's Peter's. He just doesn't know yet and I want to be the one to tell him.' I daren't tell her I suspect *he's* the one playing away. He's also the one destroying the village. What a gent.

She nods knowingly. 'Fair enough. Congratulations, though!'

A tingle spreads through me. Finally talking about my pregnancy is the best feeling ever. I desperately try to fight the urge to spill everything, but I fail miserably and sixty seconds later I have told her how far along I am, when my first scan is, even that I think I'm carrying a little girl.

Kay nods along, beaming the entire time. 'Oh, I'm so happy for you, love. You look so bloody happy!'

'I am!'

'You can tell me to sod off if you like, but I take it your fella hasn't changed his mind on the whole baby thing?'

I shake my head and sigh, slumping down in my chair where minutes before I was in bliss. 'No, he was pretty adamant.'

'I see. And now you're pregnant ...' Her accusation doesn't need to be said out loud; she knows I got myself into this mess. 'Well, honey, he loves you. There's no doubt in my mind that once he learns the truth, he'll be over the moon.'

I nod, but I don't believe a word she is saying. She didn't see how mad Peter got that day in the nursery when he told me he didn't want more children. She doesn't know how distant he's been. She has no idea how selfish he's become.

'There's something else, though,' I say, my filter very much switched off now. 'I think he's having an affair.'

CHAPTER TWENTY-ONE

I've been watching him for weeks. He thinks he's so damn clever – taking phone calls in different rooms, coming home in a different shirt he left the house in, presumably hiding evidence. Plus, he barely talks to me.

Something is going on and the only explanation is, there's someone else. More than once I have seen the initial "S" pop up on his phone. I know who it is, I'm not stupid. Sara texts him every damn day, right under my nose, and I'm sick of it.

When I first realised it was happening, I ignored it. It was like the sun – look too closely and I'd get burnt. But, now this baby is getting bigger, turning into an actual child who needs love and stability. I know I need to deal with it. I need to put a stop to it.

I have options. I could tell him about the baby in the hope he'll walk away from his new toy. I could confront him about the affair and keep quiet about the baby, at least that way I know he wants *me*. Or, I could tell him about the baby *and* that I know about the affair. Lay it all on the table and see what happens.

My head is so screwed up. I just don't know what to do. One thing I know for certain is, I need evidence. It'd be reckless to make a decision without knowing for sure what is going on with him.

He walks through the door with a huge smile on his face and I can't help but wonder if it's because he's happy to see me, or because he's had a great day shagging his mistress.

When he slips upstairs for his post-work shower, I creep into the bedroom and slide his phone out of his jacket pocket.

I tilt the screen towards the light to see where his fingers have smudged it. I can see where he taps on the screen most: 0-1-3-7.

It doesn't take a genius. Max was born on 31st July.

I tap 3-1-0-7 and clench my stomach when the screen unlocks. Bingo.

I raise my head and listen. Peter is singing *Dancing Queen*, the shower water still splashing against the glass pane. Without wasting any time, I click into his messages.

The top one is from me, telling him I can't wait to see him. I cringe at my forced soppiness to keep him sweet and move onto the next message.

"S".

He's not stupid. He's deleted the message thread. But, he hasn't had the chance to delete the one remaining message, and I read it with disgust.

I had a great day today, babe. Let me know when you've booked the hotel. Xxx

I want to be sick. I want to kick and scream. I want to ram his phone down his throat. How dare he? How dare he do this to me after promising me the world? After everything he's done to me?

The shower turns off with a rattle of the pipes and I push the phone back into his jacket pocket. I hear the bathroom door click open just as I tread off the top stair and tip-toe down before he sees me. I need to compose myself before he comes down. I'm scared of what I'll do, and I need to face this calmly.

Ten minutes later, he trots downstairs without a care in the world. 'Dinner smells good,' he says as per usual, planting a kiss on the top of my head like you would a puppy who's mastered toilet training.

'Tikka masala, your favourite,' I say. It's not his favourite, not at all, but the little dig feels good. Plus, I laced his dinner with laxatives on a whim, just to provide that extra kick. I was feeling petty. I don't know why I bother cooking for this man. What kind of idiot spends all day cooking for a man who's cheating on her? This kind of idiot, clearly.

It isn't until we're sitting in front of the TV, eating the food I have slaved over, when I finally dare say something. 'How's Sara?'

He has the nerve to look aghast. Almost disgusted. 'How am I supposed to know?'

'Oh, I just thought you'd be in touch with her, given that you share a child together.' I fight hard, but fail to keep the bite out of my voice.

'What's got into you? I don't bother with the cow unless I absolutely have to.'

Not true. Didn't Sara thank him for helping her out last time she was here? Not to mention the damn texts. 'Really?'

'Really!' His voice is raised, warning me to back off.

'Then why do I get the feeling you're not telling me something?' I can't tell him I saw the text. It's my secret ammo and I plan on whipping it out as a last resort. Hopefully, I won't need to. I don't want him to divert the focus back to me for snooping through his phone.

'Because you're fucking crazy, Jen. Always paranoid, always miserable. Give it a rest, would you?'

'How can I give it a rest if you can't keep your dick in your pants?'

My harsh words shock me, but not as much as they shock him. He stares at me, his cutlery hovering in his hands. Tikka masala slithers off his knife, dripping onto his plate. His shoulders heave with every breath and his eyes are open wide. A hot flush flashes over my entire body. I'm scared.

Without a word, he stands up, holding his dinner. He looks me right in the eye before launching the plate against the wall. Curry slips down the wallpaper, leaving a trail of brown greasy lumps of rice to slop onto the floor in slow motion. He stands there, panting, his fists clenched like it's taking every ounce of effort to stop himself from hitting me.

'I swear to God, Jen. Stop with this paranoid bullshit, or you'll be out of here so fast you won't know what's hit you.'

He heads out of the room, slamming the door behind him so hard that a picture falls off the wall and smashes with a resounding crack.

I sit in shock. His anger leaves behind a throbbing echo. Everything feels so messy. I feel so helpless.

Moments later, I hear him storm back downstairs and leave the house. His car engine roars and I hear him drive off. I've never been so glad to be without him.

Five minutes later, I'm cleaning his dinner off the floor, wondering how my life got this bad. What have I done to deserve this? All I can do is pray he ate enough laxatives to ruin his date.

I pat my belly. 'It's okay, little one. I'll figure this out.'

CHAPTER TWENTY-TWO

If Peter won't admit the truth, there's only one thing for it: catch him in the act. I'm like a woman on a mission.

I imagine what my mum would be saying to me if she could see me right now. Her sober version would have been sympathetic: 'Don't let him win, darling. You're better than this. Leave him with your head held high.' The drunk version would be far less gentle: 'Silly cow. Too weak to leave a bloke? You're pathetic.'

I obviously prefer the sober version, but I'm more inclined to believe the latter. And I pander to it. I know I should have run the second he threw the plate at the wall, but here I am – still living in his house, growing his baby, living with anxiety so high I can't sleep, I can't eat, and I can't focus.

I'm not weak, though. Stupid, maybe; but not weak. I'm standing on the street and leaning on my car, across from Sara's office. Earlier, I called the receptionist team pretending to be a business associate, to see if she was in. They transferred me through to her phone. I hung up before she answered, but now I know for sure that she's here.

Now, all I have to do is wait. I considered following Peter, but if he catches me I would have a much harder time explaining my behaviour. Besides, his work routine is so erratic (at least I think it is) that I won't know what's going on, making subtlety even more difficult. Oh, who am I kidding? He frightens me.

"S".

Lots of people have a name starting with "S". I know that, but Sara is just so obvious. The mother of his child, sexy, beautiful. "S" has to be Sara.

And there she is. She exits her office, treading down each step in stilettos with such grace that jealousy takes over me. The way she moves with a little bounce in her step is so endearing. Her long, bare legs are toned and tanned. Her makeup is immaculate and classy. Her blonde hair sweeps down her back, swaying side to side as she sashays down the road.

I cross the street, keeping my distance, and trudge along behind her. She heads along Darner Street, past all the charity shops and mobile phone stores. When she approaches Starbucks, she slows down and checks her appearance in the window reflection. She finds an invisible blemish in the corner of her eye and wipes it away with the tip of her finger before heading inside.

To see my husband. To cheat on me. To talk about whatever disgusting acts they get up to in a seedy hotel room.

I sit on a bench outside where I can spy on her over my book. I can just make out her green dress walking past the counter and she heads to the right, approaching the bay window and giving me a perfect view of her. I see a man stand up with his back to me. He pushes his chair into the glass. With his thick, black hair and pressed shirt, I have no doubt who that man is. Peter! He stands up and greets her with a hug, and I avert my eyes when he spins her and grabs her pert backside.

I can't take this anymore. If I confront them here in public, he can't retaliate with more aggression. I step into the road, narrowly avoiding a cyclist who shouts profanities at me as he continues his journey. I call out an apology, but he responds by waving his middle finger.

The coffee shop is busy, and the smell of coffee makes me nauseous, but I'm here now and I've got to see this through. The sooner this ends, the sooner this mess will go away.

Sara sees me first. 'Jen! How nice to see you.' She smiles at me with genuine warmth.

I'm thrown. What a weird thing to say to someone who's just caught you doing the dirty on her. Then, Peter turns to face me. Only, it isn't Peter. It's Harry, Laura's husband.

His mouth drops open at the sight of me. 'Jen, fancy seeing you here.' His eyes flit between me and his fancy woman. 'How do you know Sara?' He's stammering like a child who's been caught with his hand in the cookie jar.

***

'Sara is Peter's ex and the mother of his child,' I say bluntly. 'Isn't that right, Sara?'

'Yeah, Harry knows all about Max.' She smiles and goes to press her hand on his shoulder, but he leans away before her hand lands, making her stumble.

Harry is biting his lip so hard, I worry he'll chew right through it. I'm guessing he had no idea Sara was connected to Peter. 'Sara and I are colleagues,' he blurts out.

I hold in my laughter. I want to make him sweat. 'Oh? I thought you worked in the oil industry. And Sara works in event planning, right?'

'No! No, you're right. Sara is helping me plan the office Christmas party.' Harry's neck is flushed and he attempts a smile that just makes him look manic.

Sara's eyes flit between the two of us, her eyebrows pressed together. She looks as stunned as I feel. Does she not know about Laura? I can see the penny dropping as she leans back in her chair and folds her arms. She's waiting to see how this plays out and I'm more than willing to show her.

'And how's Laura, your *wife*? I haven't seen her in a while.'

'Yeah, she's good.' Before he's even finished talking, he scoops up Sara's bag and hands it to her. 'We'd better get going, lots to discuss.' Grabbing Sara's elbow, he pulls her up and towards the door, leaving their steaming drinks on the table.

I watch them leave, unease tingling my skin. Laura is a kind soul, she doesn't deserve this. She absolutely dotes on that man and he's treating her like crap. I'm tempted to call her, but destroying her marriage and ripping her family apart shouldn't be done on the phone. Plus, I get the feeling Sara is about to learn some truths and she's not the type to keep her mouth shut. Maybe I don't have to get involved.

My sympathy runs deep for Laura and I now have to carry around the weight of Harry's infidelity. Another thing I need to think about and make a decision about. I just wish I was better at dealing with confrontation.

Laura thinks her man is an absolute angel. How wrong can one person be? As I walk back to my car, I allow myself to reflect on my situation. Harry cheating on Laura hits too close to home. I always thought my relationship was unbreakable, just like Laura does. Yet, I've just witnessed how fragile her marriage truly is and it's cutting deep.

Peter may not be having an affair with Sara, but he's up to something. I'm on the cusp of a massive breakthrough and I'm utterly terrified it's going to destroy me. How could I have been so stupid to think he was so damn perfect? Of course he isn't. He's far from it.

And how could I have been so stupid as to get pregnant when he told me he didn't want a child? The red flags were flying high at that point, but I just saw them as an invitation to walk right into the battleground.

I'm a fool and I deserve everything I get.

CHAPTER TWENTY-THREE

HMRC's deadline for filing Gill's overdue tax returns is looming. They were completed almost two weeks ago, but until I find out about the fundraising income, I can't do it. I also haven't found the courage to ask her about that yet.

I have been doing a little investigation, though. I have timed my visits with various classes and counted the number of people who pay cash, and not even half of that money has made it to the spreadsheets. There was a christening party here last weekend and there's no sign of that income in the records, though I do have food receipts. It's small amounts here and there that would amount to tens of thousands of pounds over the years.

Right now, Gill's profit is massively understated, meaning her tax bill is going to be way too low. According to her bank account, she's only been paying herself minimum wage, but given the new Range Rover she's driving around in, I think Gill is actually a very wealthy woman. The whole situation is making me feel incredibly uncomfortable, so today is the day I confront Gill. I can't put it off anymore.

She arrives at the centre after me, clutching a wad of post. I've noticed she has a tendency to leave her post unopened in a drawer in the office, which might explain how she got herself in this position with the tax authorities in the first place. I wait for her to make herself a herbal tea and I decline her offer of one for me. It doesn't feel right letting her make me a drink when I am about to scare her to death. Or at the very least, cause an argument. I leave her to it, hoping the herbs in her tea are soothing.

Eventually I bite the bullet and leave the office. 'Gill, can we have a quick chat?' I ask her, pulling her attention away from rearranging the hall for the craft workshop due to start in half an hour.

She turns to me and frowns. 'Sure! But, why do you look so scared? Don't tell me HMRC has been in touch. How much is the fine?' Her eyes are wide open with panic as she heads over to me.

We head back into the office together and I frown back at her. I have always treaded carefully around the subject of HMRC, but now I don't have that luxury. This conversation needs to happen. Right now.

My tummy flutters as my little girl shifts around. It's been happening for a while now and I've noticed she only does it when I need her support. She's a little gem and she inspires me to be strong.

'They haven't,' I tell Gill. 'Though we've got to submit these forms by the end of the week, or they might not be so patient with you.'

'So, what's the problem? I've signed them off already. Submit them.' She's still holding her post and pushes the letters into the desk drawer, except for one which she fingers nervously.

'I can't, not yet.' That makes her look up. 'We need to talk about the centre's income.'

'Income? You know more than me about the numbers.'

'That's just it, I don't think I do.' I don't know how to go on. I need to be careful here. Gill might not even be aware of the "mistakes" she's been making. Maybe she doesn't view the contributions people have made as business income? She probably just thinks the cash she's pocketing is just a few pounds here and there.

I have spent some time estimating how much she could not be declaring and with the popularity of the hall and the number of years she's been doing this, the amount is eye-watering. My guess is close to fifty thousand pounds. And I worry there's more to this than meets the eye. Gill's watching me, her face a picture of confusion, fear, and annoyance.

I rip off the plaster. 'I think we've missed a number of cash transactions and I really need to report one hundred percent of the income to the tax office if I'm to do this properly.'

'What do you mean? You have all the info, Jen.'

'I don't think I do. There is a huge discrepancy. Last Thursday, for example, I noticed you took over fifty pounds from your yoga clients, but there's no record of it in your accounts. Then, there was the open day last Christmas where you asked people to donate to charity. You never made that donation, did you?'

'You think HMRC are going to care that I made a couple of mistakes? Jen, they've got bigger fish to fry.'

I take a deep breath. 'I don't think this is just a couple of mistakes, Gill. I think this has been happening for a while. I have been over and over your spreadsheets and you have expenses for days that have no income. Nothing is adding up.'

She sighs and nonchalantly peels open the envelope she's been holding, like she doesn't have a care in the world. She glances at the contents and her eyebrows crease. When she looks back at me, there's a fire in her eyes and she slams down her mug. 'What exactly are you accusing me of, here?'

'Nothing!' And it's the truth. I wanted to assume that Gill made an honest mistake, but now that I've seen her reaction, I'm not so sure.

'Well, that's not how you're coming across.'

'Sorry if I've offended you, but you hired me to do a job and it's down to me to make sure it's done right.'

'No, Jen. This isn't *right*. Accusing me of stealing isn't *right*.' Her voice has gone up an octave and her red hair seems to be standing on end.

'So, you're saying there are no missing income streams?'

'Absolutely not, and if you think you're going to stand here in *my* community centre and carry on with this nonsense, you have another thing coming. I've worked too damn hard on this place to just be insulted.' She snarls at me and turns her back. 'Get out, Jen. I'll employ someone who actually knows what they're doing.'

'You can't do that! The tax returns are due in a few days.'

'Just get out, Jen. This is my centre, and no one is going to take it away from me!' She screws up the paper she's been holding and launches it at me. It lands outside the open door.

I recoil in horror. Her aggression forces me out the door, my protestations falling on closed ears. She slams the door behind me with such force that the wall rattles.

I knew that was going to be a difficult conversation, but I naively thought we could find a resolution. As I go to leave, my foot nudges the scrunched-up paper on the floor. Curiosity gets the better of me and I scoop it up.

I get in my car and open up the letter, my fingers inexplicably trembling. The letter is branded with the owner of the building's logo. I scan the letter and raise my hand to my mouth. Gill's community centre is being pulled down. In a few weeks, the heart will be ripped out of the village. And it's all thanks to Peter.

Gill has lost everything. And when I tell HMRC of her tax evasion, she might just lose her freedom, too.

CHAPTER TWENTY-FOUR

I'm still in shock when I pull up outside my house. Everything is falling apart. Peter is slipping away, I've just lost my only source of income, and I'm clinging onto a secret too big for my fragile state to handle: my husband is a huge part of the destruction of the village. The village that has been here for hundreds of years – idyllic, quiet, blissful – is soon to be part of the rail link interchange.

The thought of how Laura, Gill, and Greg and Erin will react makes me want to vomit. What if they never speak to me again? I'll be all alone.

I step out of the car and my heart sinks when Greg comes scurrying over. I'm not in the right frame of mind for his joviality. I press my palms to my face and pray he doesn't notice I'm on the brink of collapse. I'm not prepared to talk about my feelings with this man.

'You all right, love?'

'Yeah,' I reply, edging towards my house, hoping he gets the hint. 'I'm really good, thanks. Just busy.'

He doesn't get the hint. In fact, he keeps walking towards me until he's standing far too close. 'I saw what them idiots did to your place.'

He gestures at the red paint that refuses to be removed from the front of my house. It has faded, but is still embarrassingly visible from halfway down the road.

'Yeah, little sods,' I say, unable to get the venom out of my voice.

He presses a hand on my shoulder. I long to step away, but I don't want to appear rude. It's weird seeing him without Erin by his side. 'I hate to think of you all alone and vulnerable in there. If there's anything you need, anything at all, you know where to find me, don't you?'

'Of course, and I really appreciate that, Greg. But, I really need to get inside and clean up.'

'Of course you do.' He looks me straight in the eye. 'Peter seems like the type of guy to expect a pristine home, am I right?'

'No, not at all,' I say, and it's the truth. Peter has never made demands. He has plenty of faults, but he's never been unreasonable. Has he? Not explicitly, no, but now that I think about it, he does have high standards for someone unwilling to help out around the house. 'I'd better go. Thanks again.'

To my horror, he follows me down the path. I can feel his breath on the back of my neck. 'Jen?' he murmurs into my ear.

I spin around. What does this guy want from me? 'Yes?' I snap through clenched teeth.

He looks hurt. 'Oh, don't be like that, I just want to help you.' He steps even closer, oblivious of my personal space. I try to step back again, but the wall blocks me. 'Is that fella of yours up to no good?'

'What?'

'You look upset, and I can only assume it's to do with that man of yours.'

'We're fine, thank you.'

He nods and finally steps away from me. I can breathe again.

'Just a little advice, take it or leave it: jealousy works wonders for a marriage. Trust me.' He grins at me, his lips pressing against his teeth.

'Please,' I whisper. 'I have to go.'

'I'm here if you need me.' He says before walking away, whistling a jaunty tune.

I struggle to catch my breath. I'm being silly, I must be. Greg is just overly friendly and I'm just under a lot of stress. Then why do I feel so icky? My hands are shaking so much I struggle to get the key in the keyhole. In my peripheral vision I see the net curtain next door twitch and I inwardly curse Nana's nosiness. I cannot add her to my sense of overwhelm right now. Finally, the key pushes into the tiny hole and the door flies open. I fall into the hallway, gasping for air, desperately trying to fight off the panic.

***

I'm a shell of who I used to be. It's like I've hollowed out all the stress and pain and there is simply nothing left. By the time Peter comes home, I have composed myself, but my efforts aren't as effective as I wanted them to be.

'What's wrong with you now?' Peter asks, as I'm cleaning up the kitchen after dinner.

'Nothing,' I say, refusing to meet his gaze.

'Yeah, there is something – you're in a right mood. And dinner was shit.'

I tense up. Greg may be a disgusting human being, but maybe he was right about Peter treating me like rubbish. I feel like I have been looking at him through frosted glass for the last few months and the glass is now crystal clear. I'm beginning to see his true colours, and they're ugly.

'I'm fine,' I say. 'I've just had an interesting day.' I don't know why I'm doing it, but I have the sudden urge to get a reaction out of him. 'I saw Greg today.'

'Yeah? Is he the one we had round for dinner, with his frumpy wife?'

'That's the one.' I feel bad for Erin; she's lovely and deserves more than her weird husband and Peter's insults.

'What did he want? You haven't invited them around again, have you?'

I shake my head and grab a glass off the draining board. I rub it with a tea towel and turn to face him. I want to see how he reacts. I need to see that he still cares.

'Absolutely not. Actually, he tried it on with me.' Okay, it might be a lie, but only a little one. Greg made his feelings about me known earlier.

There's a pause where I can feel the tension almost vibrate between us. Then, to my surprise, Peter laughs. His wicked laughter cuts through me like a blade. Why is this so funny to him?

'Well, you can't blame a guy for trying,' he says, rubbing his face with the palms of his hands. He sounds tired.

'Is that all you've got to say about it? What if I reciprocated his advances?'

I expect him to fly off the handle, but he doesn't even engage with me. 'Yeah, well, once a whore, always a whore.'

I drop the glass and it bounces before shattering into a million pieces. I move towards him, stepping on the shards. 'How dare you!'

'I saw you at dinner. Flirting with him. Your tits hanging out. You may as well have had a sign around your neck with "fuck me" written on it. He and his missus were on heat for you, and you lapped it up. You make me sick.'

I blink back the tears. I refuse to show any weakness. *He* is in the wrong, not me, and I will not be beaten down. 'When did you get so cruel?' I ask him, my wobbly voice betraying my resolve.

'Oh, don't do that.'

'Do what?'

'Gaslight me.'

Wait, is that what's happening here? Is this all my fault? Surely not. I think about the last few months. Peter has been cold and distant, and he's clearly having an affair; not to mention the time he forcefully had sex with me in a field.

The thought of our baby breaks me and I fall into hysterics. I'm as shattered as the glass on the floor. My sobs come in thick, noisy wails. I'm livid. I'm mourning the person I used to be, the woman who got lost amongst the lies Peter fed me.

He sneers at me as I crouch on the floor. 'You'd better clean that mess up.' Then, he turns to leave the room.

'Peter!' I call out to him, and he stops dead. 'You don't care, do you? As long as I am here playing wifey – washing your clothes, cooking your food, cleaning your home – you don't give a shit about me. Tell me, Peter, do you still love me? Have you ever loved me?'

He slowly turns to face me. His eyes pierce into me, his upper lip curled at the edges. I'm too angry to shrink away.

'You know what, Jen? I don't fucking know.'

And with that, he walks away, not a hint of emotion on his face.

CHAPTER TWENTY-FIVE

I spend the next four hours cleaning manically. I scrub every surface and corner at least twice and the house smells strongly of bleach with a hint of lemon. It's a smell that takes me straight back to my mum. Cleaning was a habit I developed to get me through her drinking binges. It gave me something to focus on that wasn't the devastation created by the one person I loved.

Peter is fast asleep when I finally go to crawl into bed in the early hours of the morning. He's snoring softly, like he doesn't have a care in the world. And, to be honest, he doesn't. He doesn't care about the village or its inhabitants. He doesn't care about his home being well-kept, because I've got that covered. And he most definitely doesn't care about me.

But now, there's not just myself to consider in all this – there are two. My little girl kicks, reminding me that I'll never be alone again. As much as I want Peter and I to work, I know now that it doesn't have to. There's a love deep in me that'll never fade, never change. It's just there, built into me, and there is nothing my little girl can do that will hurt me enough to walk away.

Unlike Peter.

I know our relationship is doomed. Do I still love him? A part of me does. But, it's a small part clinging onto the past. I feel sad for that part.

The next question I have to ask myself is, can I leave him? Or, more specifically, do I want to? I searched deep to answer this question while I cleared out the fridge. The truth is, I *do* want to leave him. I can't do this anymore. He scares me, and I can't stay just in case I get the old him back, because that would mean putting my daughter in danger. The risk is too great.

Why did he have to change? Which version of him is real? Is it the sweet, kind, gorgeous guy I first fell for? Or, is it this cruel, manipulative, nasty man lying beside me now? I roll over and sigh. Sleep isn't going to come easily tonight, of that much I can be sure.

Nerves claw at me when I think about walking away. Where would I go? The tiny inheritance I got from Mum's apartment has been spent on making this house habitable. I have no one to run to and no money to support us. The money I got from working for Gill will hardly cover the first month's rent in a tiny flat, let alone pay for everything my baby needs. I could sign up for benefits, but I've read in the forums online that it can take months and months for them to find me a council house. If ever. I curse the prenup I signed before we got married. Love makes you foolish.

I turn over again, my nose just inches away from Peter's. I grimace. I can't believe I used to think this man was attractive. His nose is too long and pointed. His lips are thin. He has wrinkles in the wrong places. Normally, wrinkles sit around the eyes and mouth, whereas his streak across his cheeks. I used to think that was endearing; now, it's ugly. To top things off, this man has turned me into a pet, a toy. A plaything he can pull out and abuse whenever he desires.

There's a scraping sound outside the bedroom. It's like something is being brushed along our bedroom door. I sit halfway up, leaning on my forearms, and listen. The sound seems to travel down the hall towards the stairs. Then, it stops, as if paused at Max's room, before carrying on.

I give Peter a shove. 'Peter,' I whisper. He opens an eye and glares at me before closing it again and rolling over. 'Peter,' I say again, sitting upright now. Footsteps creep down the stairs. Their descent is painfully slow.

I jab Peter in the ribs. My heart is hammering in my chest and for the first time in weeks, I really need him. He can't let me down this time. 'There's someone in the house,' I whisper in his ear, praying the intruder can't hear me.

Peter sits up now with shocking speed, making me fall back onto my pillow. 'Uh?' he says, far too loudly.

I point to the bedroom door. 'On the stairs.'

Peter leaps out of bed and scratches his balls as he heads over to the wardrobe. He pulls out a cricket bat.

I'm torn. I don't know whether to go with him into potential danger, or stay here and risk leaving myself vulnerable to someone else creeping in? I decide the most sensible option is to follow the man with the best and only weapon we've got.

Peter is first onto the landing, and I watch his shoulders drop when he realises there's no one there. They must have gone downstairs, and we follow suit. I grip the back of his T-shirt and squeeze tight. He peers into the living room: empty. The dining room and office: empty.

There's only the kitchen left. I look over at the kitchen door in horror. It's like time stands still as I stare into the back of my house. Smoke swirls in the moonlight. If it wasn't so horrifying, it would be beautiful. Ethereal.

Common sense finally catches up with me and I turn to run to the front of the house, but Peter keeps treading towards the kitchen and it dawns on me that there's no smell. No heat. This isn't a fire.

'Jesus Christ,' Peter admonishes, flicking on the light.

I gasp, my hands automatically reaching to the top of my head in shock. The sharp intake of breath immediately makes me cough in the powder that floats through the air.

Flour. Whoever was in here has dumped flour absolutely everywhere.

They've reached high and low to cover a spectacular amount of surface area. It's going to take me weeks to sort this out. The horror hits me like a ton of bricks. Who on Earth did this? And how did they get in?

Peter answers that one for me. 'Jen, you didn't lock the back door.' He's standing by the back door, wobbling the handle up and down to prove my idiocy.

I feel the colour drain from my face. Is this my fault? Was I really that stupid? I cast my mind back to when I came to bed. I *always* check the doors twice. First the front door, then the back. I then check the keys are on the hooks before I check the doors again. Peter always said I was obsessive, but it was just my routine and it always made sense to double-check our safety. And tonight was no exception, I'm sure of it.

But, Peter's right, there's no sign of a break-in. The key remains on the hook by the door. Was I that distracted by Peter's revelation that I forgot to lock the door?

'Call the police. Tell them how stupid you've been.' Peter says, kicking flour at me and stomping back upstairs. He leaves a trail of white footsteps behind him, then calls out from the top of the stairs. 'And lock the fucking door, will you?'

I look out into the darkness of the garden beyond. I know Peter thinks this is just a harmless prank. Or, maybe he thinks this is another incident like the graffiti – punishment for digging up countryside that surrounds the village. He thinks he's Mr Invincible. Why would it matter to him if someone was inside our home?

I know better, though. I can smell the truth. Her sickly-sweet lavender scent hangs thickly in the air, seemingly carried by the murky layer of white dust that plumes up around me as I move.

It was Nana. And, I think she's still here. I gulp down my saliva and turn around.

CHAPTER TWENTY-SIX

There's a movement outside the back door and a fearful groan escapes my lips as I step towards it, yanking it open, ready to face whatever is on the other side.

Nothing.

The garden appears clear, too, though the gate bangs in the wind, making me jump.

'Come on, baby girl,' I whisper to my tummy. I brace myself and head to the gate where I slam the bolt shut. Did I lock this earlier? I can't be sure. But, I can't remember the last time I *unlocked* it, either.

No, this gate was locked, I'm sure of it. Can Nana really be that agile to climb over? What is going on here?

I jog back into the house and triple-check the key is turned and removed from the lock. I do the same with the front door before wiping my dusty feet on the mat and heading back upstairs to climb into Max's bed.

I'm fuming. There was someone in our house and Peter's reaction was to call me stupid and go back to bed.

I roll over and squeeze my fists so tight my nails dig into my palms. I'm done with this. I'm done with everyone taking me for a ride. Gill accused me of being crap at my job when she's blatantly up to no good. Peter takes me for granted every single day, and to top things off, Nana is playing with me.

No, that's it. I'm telling Peter about the baby and giving him an ultimatum. He can either change and be the husband and father we deserve, or I'm gone. I'm now hoping it's the latter. My dream of happy-ever-after has shifted, and it looks different now.

My stomach gurgles noisily. It's my nerves. I know this isn't going to be easy, but I'll figure it out. Surely, Peter won't just let me leave with nowhere to go? He has to support me financially. Doesn't he? Surely even a prenup cannot stop me claiming child support. But, would it be enough to get settled somewhere else?

Thoughts swirl around my brain. One minute, I'm high as a kite imagining a new start and the next, I'm wracked with panic at the practicalities of it all. When I roll over again, I hear birdsong. A new start is on the horizon, and I'm going to take full advantage of it.

***

'I think you should call in sick today,' I tell Peter. I abandoned sleep in favour of cleaning the flour in the kitchen, so by the time Peter is showered and dressed the house is practically back to normal. And my hoover looks ready for the bin.

'Why would I do that?' He looks both confused and annoyed, exactly as I expected.

'We need to talk.'

He tuts. 'Not today, Jen. I'll call a locksmith and get the locks changed. You'll be fine.'

'It's not that,' I say, but that's not entirely true. I don't think I'll feel safe in this house ever again.

'Right, well you've got two minutes before I need to leave. What do we need to talk about?'

'Peter, I'm pregnant.'

The clatter of Peter's laptop bag hitting the floor makes me wince. Then, silence surrounds us and I take deep breaths, waiting for him to come to his senses. He stands staring at me, eyes wide open like I've suddenly grown an extra limb.

'No.'

Who knew such a small word could have such huge implications?

'Yes,' I reply, refusing to lower my gaze. He turns his eyes to my stomach like he can see straight into me. I place my hand over my baggy top, on my baby, suddenly conscious of how precious she is; of how my sole job in life is to protect her.

His lip curls up in a sneer and he nods his head to the side. 'Who's the daddy, Jen-Jen?' His tone makes me catch my breath. His voice is deep with mockery and his fingers are twitching at his sides.

'Don't insult me,' I say, trying to sound calm and brave, but I'm so afraid every inch of my body is willing me to run in the opposite direction. 'The baby is yours, Peter. I think she was conceived the day we went for that picnic.'

He has the audacity to look confused. Has he really forgotten about the moment my entire world shifted? When he *raped* me. Yes, I know what it was. No matter how much I've tried to ignore it, the truth has a tendency to keep hurling itself at you until you're forced to confront it. Deep sadness is suffocating me. It's like I can't look at it directly. I can only peer at it from the corner of my eye, in case it engulfs me.

My child is the product of a sexual attack.

And as much as I can never love him again, I will love her forever.

I want him to react. I need to see how he responds because this will speak volumes. His anger is exactly what I need to find the courage to leave him. The last straw.

But, he surprises me.

'Oh, Jen-Jen, why didn't you tell me before?' He pulls out a stool and plonks himself down. Every bit of energy he had has evaporated. 'You must be pretty far along?'

'The twelve-week scan is tomorrow.'

He blows air out between his teeth and runs his fingers through his hair. 'Can I come with you?' He sounds so small, so pathetic.

I want to say no just to hurt him, but I know I just don't have it in me to be that cruel. 'Of course,' I breathe. 'You're her daddy.'

'Her?'

'I have a feeling it's a girl.' I can't help but smile. I know he's been a bad man, but I can't bring myself to walk away when he's just found out the truth. I need to give him the chance to adjust to this life-changing revelation. He can change. He *has* to change if he wants us to figure this out.

'I'll call the office. Take a couple days off.'

His reaction wasn't the ecstatic response I once dreamed of, but it wasn't as violent as I was afraid of, either. It's like all life has been taken out of him. He's given up hope of his bachelor lifestyle, with his built-in housekeeper and sex toy at home. He slowly lifts himself from his seat, clutching his phone in his hand. I creep after him and watch him walk upstairs. To my horror, I notice a tear slipping down his cheek. I've broken him and I am truly devastated. I really thought he'd love our baby as much as I do.

I can't leave things like this, so I follow him upstairs. We need to talk about this properly. I need to help him see sense.

His voice drifts through the bedroom door into the hallway. I stop to listen, unwilling to interrupt. 'Sorry, babe, we're off today.'

My heart stops.

'I know, something's come up.'

A pause.

'No, everything's fine. I'll call you later and we'll arrange a new date.' He chuckles. 'You know I like the red lace. It makes you look extra naughty.'

No. I can't do this anymore. I've been a fool. I'm done. He is welcome to his bit on the side. I'm taking my baby and getting as far away from this toxic beast as I possibly can. I just need to figure a way out.

CHAPTER TWENTY-SEVEN

Considering how terrible yesterday went, it is a pleasant surprise when Peter brings me breakfast in bed this morning. He has even pulled the little teapot out from the back of the cupboard to bring me a cute pot of tea. Next to my toast, he's placed a carnation that he presumably picked from the garden.

It's a nice gesture, but it's too little, too late.

I eat heartily anyway, as the baby is particularly hungry this morning. I read over my letter from the hospital so I know where to go for my scan today. I push all thoughts of Peter away and focus on the butterflies in my belly. Today, I get to see my little baby for the first time. I get to see her little legs and arms. I get to see her beautiful face.

Amongst my excitement is the inevitable worry that I imagine must follow every mum around from the second they discover they're pregnant. What if there's something wrong? With the amount of stress I have been under lately, it would hardly be surprising and I feel sick at the thought. I push my fears aside. I can't add to my stress by worrying about something I can't control. Positive thoughts only.

Peter takes my hand as we wind our way around the hospital corridors in search of the antenatal clinic. He squeezes it so tight it hurts.

We finally reach the waiting room and give the kind-looking lady our details before attempting to get comfortable on vomit-green-coloured plastic chairs. We don't say a word to each other, but from the way he keeps shifting in his seat, I can tell he has a thousand thoughts running through his head.

By the time the sonographer calls us into a little room, his tension has built up and rather than greet her with his usual charismatic smile, he can only stare out the window.

She senses the strain between us and strokes my shoulder encouragingly. 'I'm Kendall, it's a pleasure to meet you. And how are you doing today? Are you feeling okay?'

I nod. 'I feel really strong.' It's the truth and I hope Peter picks up on my mood. I'm not going to let him walk all over me anymore. I just want to get this done so I can start to focus on providing the kind of life my baby deserves.

'That's good to hear!' She sounds genuinely pleased. She guides me to a bed and asks me to pull my top up as she taps a few keys on the intimidating ultrasound machine. 'And how's daddy?' She throws a look at Peter.

'I'm okay.'

She smiles at him in an attempt to calm his nerves. 'Don't worry, it's perfectly normal to be worried. Today should put those worries to rest.' She gives the bottle she's holding a sharp shake and squirts the sloppy gel all over my stomach. I wince unnecessarily – the gel is warm. How lovely.

A tension hangs in the air while Kendall moves her magic wand over my abdomen, her long nails tapping at various keys and swishing across the little roller ball in the middle of the keyboard. I will her to hurry up.

'So, Jen, now I'm going to turn the speaker on.'

The gentle thud of my baby's heartbeat fills the room and fills my own heart. Every second of doubt and pain I have ever experienced washes away in that instant. Nothing matters anymore. Love rushes through me, making goosebumps erupt over every inch of me and I tremble from head to toe.

Peter rushes over and clutches my hand and Kendall beams at us. 'Meet your baby! A perfectly healthy baby.'

I break down. Every last drop of pain pours out of me and I let it go, cleansing myself with the good news. I have a perfectly healthy baby.

Kendall slips out of the room and Peter, for the first time in a long time, engulfs me in a tight hug. His arms offer solace amongst the chaos and I allow myself to cry on him, my tears darkening his shirt.

'We can do this,' Peter whispers. He sounds so sincere it makes me wail more. It's only when I have calmed down a little that Peter dares to speak again. 'I mean it, Jen-Jen. It's time we stepped back into the relationship we once had. I don't know how things got so *messy*.'

Me neither. I have spent weeks blaming Peter, but it can't all have been him. One person can't create so much pain alone. I must have contributed somehow.

Peter is right. It's time we put everything behind us and see this as an opportunity to strengthen our relationship. I just hope our baby can be the glue we so desperately need. I nod at him, determined to move on from this and create the little family I have always dreamed of. I'll figure out a way to push my hate aside. I have to now, for the sake of my child.

Our baby's heart still beats in my ears. It's a glorious sound that fills me with resolve. 'Peter, are we going to be okay?'

'Yes, yes we are.' He kisses me tenderly on my forehead. 'I'm going to fix things, I promise.'

And the silly thing is, I really want to believe him.

***

I leave the hospital clutching Peter's hand, a roll of pictures of our baby in my other hand. My heart sings with joy.

Two legs. Two arms. Perfectly proportioned. A beautiful baby.

I have my man by my side. My only regret is I didn't tell him sooner. He's been so wonderful and if I had said something weeks ago, our relationship may not have snowballed like it has and he might not have cheated on me.

Don't get me wrong, I am not naive enough to think everything is automatically better. We're far too damaged for that. But, what I have now that I didn't before is *hope*. Everything might just be okay. For now, I'm just going to let myself bask in this bliss. I have spent far too much time in a state of extreme stress lately and I owe it to myself and my baby to live in this sweet moment.

When we return to the car, Peter holds my door open and helps me into my seat, like I'm a fragile doll. I let him, relishing his tender touch. He makes sure my seatbelt is secure before pushing my door shut. As he drives us out of the overcrowded car park, I stare at my baby photos. You can just make out her tiny toes and full lips. She's curled up into a little ball, loving the warm, cosy home I have made for her. She senses my love and flutters inside me as I stroke the bottom of my tiny bump, desperate to connect with her.

'Jen,' Peter hesitates.

I look up at him. His entire body is tense, and his nostrils flare furiously. His lips are pressed together, and I swear I can see the blood vessels bursting in his eyes. 'Yes?' I ask, though I'm not sure I want to have this conversation.

'I need to be honest with you.'

God, no. This isn't the time to talk about his affair. He is not going to strip away my sense of bliss. 'Not now, Peter.'

'No, I have to get this off my chest.'

'Please, not now.'

He sighs loudly through clenched teeth and always needing to get his own way, continues to blurt out whatever poison he wants to spill. 'Jen, I ...'

He doesn't get the chance to finish. The last thing I remember is hearing screaming – my own. Then seeing a tree rushing towards the bonnet.

CHAPTER TWENTY-EIGHT

My head is pounding. It's like there's a rave going on in the centre of my brain. I squeeze my eyes shut even tighter, willing the agony to go away.

I need water.

I lift my hand to reach over to my bedside table, but my action is inhibited by wires.

Where am I?

My eyes refuse to open and I have to lie back on the soft pillow and engage the part of my brain that manages my facial features. I breathe in deeply and count, slowly.

Then, the pain hits me.

It's like my body has been crushed. My left arm feels too stiff, like someone is pinning it down, and there's a strange smell of disinfectant and something I can only describe as musty decay.

My memories come pouring in.

The accident.

A cry escapes me, making me jump, as I remember the huge tree hurtling towards us, Peter crying out as his foot hammered against the brake pedal in vain. My body being thrust forward, the relief and shock when the airbag stopped me from smashing my head into the dashboard.

'You're okay, my darling. You're in the hospital, and we're taking care of you.' The nurse's voice is so soft and gentle, making my heart catch in my throat.

'P—, Pet—,' I stammer. My mouth feels disgusting and dry. My throat is too swollen to even swallow.

'Peter? Your husband is okay, my darling. You don't need to worry about him.'

I cast my eyes downwards to survey the damage. My arm is in a cast which explains the strange tightness to it. My skin is bluish, interspersed with purple blotches. The bulk of the pain is in my face and I dread looking in the mirror.

There is also a deep ache in my abdomen.

Oh, no. No, no, no.

The kind nurse is watching me, sympathy pouring from her eyes. When she sees me grab my belly, she strokes my hair. 'Now, now, dear.'

'Is she okay?'

'She?'

I want to scream. She knows exactly who I am damn well talking about.

Peter enters the room. He has a nasty gash across his forehead, held together with a neat row of stitches. He's limping and sporting a few bruises of his own, but otherwise looks unharmed.

His eyes tell me everything. They search into my soul, desperately trying to find the words that will destroy me.

My baby died.

My grief engulfs me, dragging all the air out of my lungs. I'm disconnected from the noises falling out of my mouth. I don't know what's happening to me. My body feels empty, heavy, tense. I don't know where to put my limbs and my hands flail around, reaching for the unknown source that can take away my pain.

I want my baby back.

Peter's arms reach for me, pulling me to him. I can smell his aftershave and it makes me feel sick. I try to push him away, but he clings on tighter while I pummel his chest, screaming into him.

This is too much. Is it possible for pain to physically destroy you? It's like I am broken and despite Peter desperately trying to keep my pieces together, I am dripping through his hands.

We sit like that forever. People come and go. A doctor explains to me what has happened, but I only hear five of his words.

I'm sorry for your loss.

It might have taken minutes, but it was probably hours until my cries stopped. I've run out. I'm empty. Peter is still holding me. He's a little more relaxed now and is stroking my hair.

The doctor who explained my miscarriage walks into the room, looking more dishevelled than earlier. He must have had a difficult shift. Despite all that is happening to me, I feel for him. This can't be an easy job.

'We need to discuss the next steps,' he says, getting straight to the point and letting his facial expressions offer the utmost sympathy. He is clutching a board and pulls over a chair to be near me. His voice is soft and soothing. It's hard to guess his age, but I put him at a few years older than me. He's certainly ten times the *person* I will ever be. I can't even grow a baby inside my womb, the most natural thing in the world.

I struggle to form words, so Peter speaks for me. 'What are the next steps?'

I don't want to hear the answer. I just want to go home and cry for my little baby. Cry for me.

'We need to perform a surgical procedure called dilation and curettage. Essentially, it involves clearing your womb to prevent any complications from your miscarriage.'

I nod along like this is all okay. He goes on to explain how they're going to scrape my baby out of me like cake batter. I'm shaking violently.

'You will be sedated the whole time and the procedure itself won't last more than ten minutes. Then, if all goes to plan, and I don't see why it wouldn't, you can go home in the morning.' He almost smiles, before he realises this is not the time for optimism.

I keep nodding. I nod through signing whatever forms I am given. I nod through the nurse taking my blood pressure. I nod as I wave goodbye to Peter. I nod as they take away my only hope of happiness.

CHAPTER TWENTY-NINE

To Peter's credit, he's been a gem these last three weeks. When not at work, he's doted on me as far as he's capable of doting on anyone. He's ordered my favourite food in, spooning it straight into my mouth when I've been too weak to eat. He's dressed me on the rare occasion I wanted to change into a different set of pyjamas. He's come home from work on time, every single day.

As sweet as he's been, it hasn't escaped my notice that his mourning of our baby ended just days after the accident and his patience with me, although lasting longer than I would have thought, is starting to wane.

I don't care. I don't care if he's fed up with me. I also don't care that he's seeing someone else. He thinks he's so clever. Or, maybe he thinks I am so consumed by grief that I don't notice him taking calls in the other room. I watch him re-enter the room with a red tinge to his cheeks and smelling of guilt. He doesn't meet my eye. But then, he never does anymore.

Like I said before the accident, he's welcome to his bit on the side. He can take care of me for as long as he can manage, just like I have babysat him for our entire relationship. He can give something back. Then I'm leaving. I will file for a divorce. I don't care about the house anymore. I have no love for him, and there's no baby to provide a connection.

I'm done.

Amongst the sadness for my loss, there's an anger that boils with such intensity it's frightening. If I unleash this fury on Peter, there is a high possibility that he'll react with violence. I see right through him now. Ripping down the curtains in the nursery, throwing a plate against the wall, raping me. How long is it until he throws his fists about as well? I'm at the end of my tether. My rage simmers, a constant threat to my safety.

I flick the kettle on and head into the living room while it boils. I have been trying to lose myself in a book this week in a desperate attempt to let go of my grief, just for a moment. But, I can't seem to focus on the words. Each day I try a new book, but I'm yet to find one that sweeps me away, so I poke around the bookcase to see if any of Peter's sci-fi novels tickle my fancy.

Then, something catches the corner of my eye and I turn to face the window. Nana is outside. Her hand is raised to her brow and she squints through the net curtain. A fire rages through me, starting from my toes and surging to my scalp. I charge out of the room to the front door. I fling the door open, making Nana take a step back, clutching her chest.

'You startled me!' she says. I can't believe she has the nerve to sound annoyed at me.

'Get away from my house!' I scream.

She looks baffled and steps back, stumbling over the pebbles on the drive as I step out of the house towards her.

'Can you just leave me alone? Haven't you done enough damage?' I'm screaming. There's a huge part of me pleading for me to stop, but the angrier side of me just keeps going. I unleash every ounce of hurt onto her. Even when she starts crying, I can't back off. My yelling gets louder, more desperate. I'm not even making sense anymore.

'Oi!' Kay calls out from next door. 'What the fuck do you think you're doing?' She stomps over and drapes an arm around Nana's shoulders. She pulls the old, fragile-looking woman close to her chest, sheltering her from my barrage of abuse. It's like she's comforting one of her children, not a cat-murdering old bat who needs to learn to keep herself to herself.

'That woman is insane and I've had enough!' My last word comes out as a screech and immediately all energy leaves my body. I'm drained. My legs give way and I flop to the ground in a heap of shame. Sobs wrack my entire body. What am I doing? Who have I become?

Nana turns away from Kay's chest and looks down at me. She holds her hand out to comfort me, but Kay pushes it away and instructs her to go inside. She slinks off with not a hint of expression on her face. It's like she's already forgotten my outburst. Her innocence breaks me down all the more.

Kay sits next to me, cross-legged on the ground. She doesn't touch me, her distaste for me clearly written all over her face. 'You can't just do that. You can't treat her like shit just because she's old and confused.'

'No, it's not that. I ...'

'I know you believed the lies about her. Everyone does. But, Jen, you've got to believe me, she wouldn't hurt a fly. You don't have to be frightened of her.'

I shake my head. My broken arm aches and I pull it close to me with my good arm. We sit in silence. I don't know what to say.

'Tell me what happened,' Kay finally says, though she still sounds furious.

'She was just looking through the window and I saw red.'

'No, not Nana. What's going on with *you*? A little old lady hasn't done this to you; there's got to be more to it.'

I breathe deeply and nod. My hand is drawn to my belly where my little girl used to grow. Kay notices and her facial features shift, one by one, as she connects the dots.

'Oh, darling.' She scoops me into a tight hug. She feels soft and warm and I sink myself into her sympathy. I'm reminded of my mum. I don't cry. For the first time in a long time, I feel soothed. 'I'm assuming it was the car accident? Erin told me about it, but I didn't want to just come round and ask. I figured you'd need some space.'

I nod. Coming home from the hospital with my arm in a cast caused a ripple of questions in the village, and it seems the news has spread to Kay, too.

'I'm so sorry, hun. There's no pain like it, eh?'

I glance at her. Kay has been here, too? As much as it hurts to know she has also felt like this, I feel slightly glad that she understands my anguish. I feel less alone. We share our stories, and each word muttered feels cathartic. Kay listens with such intensity and I feel a deep pleasure in getting closer to her.

The chat moves onto Peter. 'How did he take it?' Kay asks me.

I shrug. I don't want to talk about him. I'm done thinking about that man.

Thankfully, Kay picks up on the vibe and places a hand on my knee. 'If you ever need somewhere to go, come to mine, yeah? No questions asked. Day or night.'

My eyes meet hers. What does she know?

'The walls are thin,' she says simply. 'Has he hurt you?'

I shake my head, but it's a lie. He may not have caused any physical harm, but the pain he has caused me has been immense.

'Jen, I'll be honest with you. If I ever think you're in any real danger, I will be straight on the phone to the police.'

'I'm okay,' I tell her. 'Peter is hard to get along with, but I've got this.'

'Have you, though? Because a lot of women say that and they're really, *really* not okay.'

'No, I am,' I look her in the eye with a steely glare. I need Kay to know that I'm strong. 'Kay, I'm not sticking around for one second longer than I have to. I just need a job and somewhere to go.'

'Well, get a move on. I'm scared for you. And you look terrible.'

She's right. I have lost a worrying amount of weight these last few weeks. My pregnancy hid it before, but now ... Well, now I look gaunt and bony. My eyes are sinking into my head and my hair is permanently greasy. I smell, too – my depression has stopped me showering. There's even dirt under my nails.

'Don't worry about me. I'll get it together.'

'Right, well you know where I am.' She lifts herself off the ground with a moan. 'Oh, and Jen, as sorry as I am for your loss, if you ever speak to Nana like that again I won't be so understanding next time.'

She walks away, ignoring my apologies, and I'm left with a strange mix of guilt and strength. A curious concoction that lights a fire inside of me. Things need to change *now*, and I'm damn well going to sort this out.

CHAPTER THIRTY

I have been pacing the house all week trying to come up with a plan to get me out of this dire situation, and I feel like I'm about to snap. I need some space to think, so I grab my grubby trainers from the bottom of my wardrobe and head outside for a walk. Fresh air feels like the perfect antidote to my bad mood.

Peter didn't come home last night. He didn't bother telling me, either. It didn't take him long to slip back into his old ways. But, I just don't care. The only thing that bothered me is he didn't tell me, so I couldn't relax not knowing if I had the house to myself or not.

I haven't texted him. What's the point? I hope he's had a lovely time with his girlfriend. Maybe if I let him think he's got one over on me, a sliver of guilt will pull at him and he'll offer me some money to leave in peace. I smile at my silliness. That's never going to happen. Peter is too much of a selfish jerk. He'll probably move his new girlfriend in the second I've packed my bags.

The summer weather is holding strong for mid-September. The sun is beating down and a slight breeze brings a chill to the air. I breathe in deeply, holding on to the sense of calm that has overcome me. I feel like I'm grasping at the edges of a plan, and it all depends on how next week goes. I have a job interview. I have already chatted to the manager of the accountancy practice, and we got along really well, so I have high hopes. My relief is astronomical until my nerves about starting a new job take over and drag me back down to fear.

I have also applied to the council for a bedsit. The woman at the Citizens Advice Bureau told me women who are victims of domestic violence get priority, so I have that up my sleeve if need be. Peter is abusive and if he's willing to dish that card out, then I'm willing to use it against him.

Once I am settled, I'm going to save as much as I can to have IVF treatment. My little baby was a treasure and she taught me that nothing is more important to me than being a mummy. I don't need a man in my life to realise that dream when I am more than capable on my own.

I am taking steps forward and it feels incredible. I can't help walking with a skip in my step as I venture through the sleepy village. My thoughts keep racing around my head, but it feels like there's a little more space up there now to let them dance more freely.

I head to the community centre, and I'm dismayed to find some of the windows are smashed and there's a notice on the door to say the rail link initiative has planning permission to demolish the building. At least no one has realised Peter's part in all this, yet.

'Jen! Long time no see!'

I turn to see Laura with her son, Elijah, walking towards me. Laura's long, perfectly curled hair is flying in the wind. She's wearing a gleaming smile and her eyes twinkle at me. She's like a princess and I immediately feel self-conscious in my jogging bottoms, hoodie, and trainers.

Laura doesn't seem to notice my scruffiness and greets me with a tight hug. 'How are you doing?' She eyes my broken arm. I ditched the sling a while ago, but sadly there isn't much I can do about the cast. 'Been in the wars, I see.'

'Car accident.' I don't know why I said that. Of course she already knows, and her sympathetic head tilt proves it.

'Oh, I was so sorry to hear about that. It must have been terrifying.' Her eyes are wide open, and I resist the urge to laugh. *Terrifying* feels utterly ridiculous for what I've been through.

'I'm on the mend,' I say, surprised at my dismissiveness of the worst day of my life. 'How are you doing?'

'Elijah, don't get too close, it might not be safe!' Laura calls out to her son who is peering into the community centre windows. Laura may as well have not said anything, with the amount of attention he gives her request. She turns back to me. 'Yeah, we're good. Harry is back from a business trip tomorrow, so we're heading to London for the weekend. Spend some quality time together.'

My cheeks feel hot and I turn away, unable to look her in the eye, knowing Harry is having an affair. Or, was having. I'm hoping he called it quits with Sara after I caught him in the act. I doubt it, though – his arrogance is on par with Peter's.

I watch Elijah edge around the building out of sight and I toy with the idea of telling Laura. If I tell her, I will be tearing her to pieces. And maybe she already knows? Harry is away *a lot*. You can't tell me her mind hasn't wandered to the worst. Is it my place to say anything? Is it my place to *not* say anything?

'Everything all right?' Laura asks kindly. 'You look a little pale.'

'I'm fine,' I assure her. 'I've just got a lot on my plate at the minute.'

Laura continues to stare at me, the nosy cow refusing to give up on squeezing info out of me.

I fold. 'Laura, I saw Harry in Starbucks a few weeks ago.'

Laura shrugs and laughs. 'I keep telling him he'll put on weight if he keeps buying those creamy coffees, but he won't listen.'

'No, Laura. Listen ... I saw him with another woman.'

I don't tell her it was Sara. She might think I'm just doing this to rock the boat. The jealous new wife trying to push out the ex.

Her smile falters slightly before she regains her composure and forces the smile back into position. 'It was probably a business associate. Harry's a busy man.'

'That's not how you behave with a business associate, Laura.' We pause as Laura processes this information. 'I'm so sorry, but your husband is having an affair.'

She gulps. 'You're talking shit,' she snarls, her words hitting me with a force that makes me step back. 'Just because your relationship is as fake as Gill's identity, doesn't mean you can drag everyone else down with you.'

What? What did she mean by that?

Before I have a chance to respond, she stomps over to the community centre. 'Elijah?' she calls out. 'Time to go!'

Nothing. She rounds the side of the building. When she reappears around the other side of the building, her eyes are wet. 'I can't find him!'

Our disagreement is immediately put aside. I go to search the woods behind the building, but there's no sign of him. Laura calls his phone and a rap tune blares out from next to a bench by the huge bins. Laura walks over and scoops up the phone. Her skin is pure white.

'It's Elijah's.' Her voice wobbles and she swallows back her sheer terror.

'We'll find him,' I say with as much certainty as I can muster. But, if Thistlewood has taught me anything, nothing is ever good news in this godforsaken village.

CHAPTER THIRTY-ONE

Two hours later, the police have organised a search of the local area. Locals call out Eljah's name all around me. I can hear them from streets over, by the canal, checking the parks.

I feel like I'm having an out-of-body experience. One minute he was there, the next he just wasn't. Someone can't just vanish into thin air.

I don't know where to go. I volunteered to search the residential streets, but where do I start? I see Laura sitting on a bench outside the community centre, in floods of tears, and I just feel utterly hopeless. This is my fault. I distracted her when she should have been watching her son. We need to find him, and soon, or I'll never forgive myself.

I see Greg over the road, walking in the opposite direction with a determined look on his face. He throws me a grim smile and I wave back warily, and we continue our personal missions to find Elijah, our previous encounter put aside in light of the situation.

I tentatively head down the road, letting my feet guide the way without any intervention from my brain. It feels good to be taking action and my pace quickens.

'Elijah!?' I call out, immediately feeling silly. Why would he respond to me when he's clearly ignoring everyone else? That's if he can even hear us ...

I walk past people arriving home from work, unaware of the missing child, and looking confused by the hustle and bustle. A couple come forward to see what is happening and once learning the circumstances, immediately join in the search. Thistlewood really does have a good community spirit.

I wander around feeling like a pointless fool. Panic is welling up in my chest and it isn't until I am standing at the end of my road that I realise where I am. It's a small cul-de-sac, so no one has thought to look down here, and the quietness is unnerving. I walk towards my house; towards Nana's house.

Nana can't have anything to do with this, can she? I tell myself she's an innocent, old lady – why would she, and *how* would she, take a ten-year-old boy from under our noses? Elijah might be small for his age, but I'm certain he could still overpower a woman who can barely stand up straight. And surely, he'd just scream if a creepy old woman tried to snatch him.

But, then I remember what she did to Oliver. I saw the state of my kitchen after she broke in. I know she can survive the coldest of February nights in just a nightie. She's harder than she looks. And harder than she pretends to be.

When I'm about a hundred yards away from my drive, I stop dead. Nana is standing in her window, her arms dangling at her sides and her eyes burning into mine. I want to turn away from her icy stare, but I know I must stand up to this woman. I can't let her wreck my life when Peter is already having such a good go at that himself.

I walk closer, determined to speak to Nana to find out what she knows. But, as I approach, she raises the palm of her hand, forcing me to stop. She isn't just staring, she's imploring me. She looks frightened and her fear feeds mine.

I tip my head to the side and shrug to try and get her to tell me what's wrong, and she just points to her right, towards my house. Her eyes flick in the same direction.

She wants me to go home. What has she done now? What lies in wait for me there?

I hesitate. Do I go? I really want to go and find a police officer and ask them to enter first, but that seems ludicrous given they're currently searching for a missing child. Plus, how could I tell them I'm scared of an old woman and my own home?

No, I need to put my big-girl pants on and check for myself. I can handle Nana. And once I've dealt with whatever she has done, I'm reporting her. She can't keep getting away with causing chaos.

I throw Nana a dirty look, hoping I look strong, and take my key out of my pocket. My hand trembles as I insert it into the keyhole. Why am I so on edge? It's as if the threshold to my house wraps me in a tension I can't shrug off.

The house is quiet, and I stand at the open door, waiting for whatever lies in wait to jump out at me. What has she done this time? I have no more pets to murder. Has she trashed my kitchen again? Maybe she's left me a gift in the toilet? I smirk to myself at that one and my heart rate slows down a little.

I throw my handbag down on the floor, not bothering to tuck it into the cupboard under the stairs.

Someone coughs.

A woman.

In the living room.

But, if Nana is in her house, who is in mine?

I'm tempted to run, but I'm more compelled to find out what's going on. To put an end to this, once and for all.

I round the corner into the living room.

'Erin?'

She's standing in the centre of the room, a smile on her face, her eyes glinting like she's keeping a secret.

'How did you get in here?' I ask.

Her smile grows wider, and she waves a key at me. 'I pinched it from the little key bowl in the hall when we came for dinner. It really is a silly idea to keep all your spare keys in the same place.'

She's right, of course. But, why did she take a key?

'What do you want, Erin?' Despite her smile, there's a glint in her eyes that injects terror into my core. Whatever this is, it's not good news.

'Oh, nothing, dear,' she says, trying and failing to keep a straight face. Eventually, she gives up and chuckles. 'Oh, pish. Actually, I want quite a lot.' She inches towards me with her arms outstretched and for the first time, I notice she's clutching a length of rope.

I dart back, but Erin is too quick for me. My scream is immediately muffled by the impact of her fist. My limbs are everywhere, completely out of my control, and Erin is both faster and stronger than me. She pushes me over the arm of the sofa before jumping on my back to pin me down. My broken arm pushes into the harder surface below the cushions and pain ricochets through my upper body and emanates out of my mouth as a scream.

Erin silences me by smashing my face into the cushion, threatening me with suffocation, and I soon stop screaming when I start to feel dizzy. I hear my cast crunch under the tight cord as she binds my hands behind my back. When she's satisfied I'm at her mercy, she sits me up like a doll and continues to tie my ankles together. I'm powerless. I'm scared.

'Erin, please, what's happening?'

She strokes my hair and sighs. 'You've been chosen, my darling.'

'Chosen for what?'

Her smirk is more terrifying than my constraints. 'Greg likes to play with toys. I like to watch. And you, my dear, are a toy.'

My breath is swept away by her sinister words. *Play?* Play how? I wrack my brain for the answer that will make all of this make sense. Erin, to my horror, answers my unspoken questions.

'We like you, Jen. You should feel at least a little bit flattered. You're a beautiful woman. You being married to that *fool* just made our decision final. Greg will be here soon in the van, then when it gets dark, we'll take you to the playhouse. You'll like it, it's cosy and fun.' She stops and grins at me as if she's letting me play a fun game of Monopoly. 'The last one didn't think so, though. She didn't last long, but something tells me you'll go for much longer.'

'What did you do to her?' I ask, though I'm not sure I want the answer. My hands are fiddling at the knots behind my back, but Erin is clearly skilled at binding people.

She shrugs and leans back against the fireplace, wobbling the Buddha she and Greg bought me. 'Every man has sexual needs, Jen. You know that. Isn't that why you've let Peter sleep with his plaything for so long?'

'How ... how do you know about that?'

'Don't interrupt me,' she snaps. 'Greg, like any man, has sexual needs. His are just more ... *aggressive*. He gets sexual pleasure out of extreme pain and I can't exactly provide him that, can I? It wouldn't be healthy for our marriage. So, we have an agreement. I provide his toys and he stays with me, providing for me. Plus, I get to watch, which I must admit is terribly exciting.'

I try to pull my hands apart and I feel the rope give by just a few millimetres.

'Oh, there's no point fighting it, dear. This isn't my first rodeo.' She laughs again and I groan through the urge to wrap my fingers around her neck. She walks over to the window. 'It's just bloody typical that Elijah, that little shit, picked today to wander off. The streets are crawling with police.'

'You've got nothing to do with Elijah's disappearance?'

She looks disgusted. 'Of course not. Greg isn't a paedophile, Jen. What a horrible thought.'

I hear voices approaching the house and I take my chance to scream. The second the sound erupts from my lips, Erin runs over to me, pushes me down and sits on my head, her large backside denying me oxygen. 'Come on, Jen, I thought you'd be more sensible than this. If you're a good girl, Greg might go a bit easier on you, you know? He likes his girls to do as they're told – it makes him stay a little calmer. I mean, one girl donkey-kicked him right in the balls once when he was mounting her from behind. That didn't end well. I'll let you use your imagination with that one.' She shivers, but it's a mockery, and I can tell she enjoyed it. She continues. 'Now. Can I trust you, or should I shove something in that pretty little mouth of yours?'

I buck my body upward, my only way to communicate with Erin that her message has been understood. I'll be good. At least until I figure this out.

Erin steps away and sits me back up to look at me. I'm panting through my tears. She gently tucks my hair behind my ear. 'Good girl.' Her hand runs down my cheek and she lets it rest on my breast. 'Greg is going to love you.'

When Erin forced me down, my cast wedged itself under the rope, giving me a little slack to work with. I might just have a chance. I need to buy time to pull the ropes apart. 'How many?' I ask. 'How long?'

'Oh, decades, my darling. As for how many? I have no idea. We used to go on holiday to source our girls; it was much easier to remain undetected when we kept moving. But, we've been feeling our age lately and holidaying just feels like too much of a chore. So, we started selecting from the local pool of sweeties.'

My lips curl. 'You two are responsible for women disappearing across the county.'

'Some of them, yes. Not all. And not all of our girls are picked up by the media. It's funny how the press picks and chooses who to make a big deal of. The prettier ones tend to make a splash in the headlines.'

'You'll never get away with this.' The cliché is ridiculous. Especially when I have no real plan for escape.

Erin looms over me, fury pouring through her widened eyes. 'Well, we were just bloody fine until your bastard husband came along.'

Peter? What has he got to do with this?

'We know who he is, Jen. Proposing that damn train line to come right through this village, digging up the woods, unearthing all kinds of horrors.'

'You buried the girls in the woods?'

'Why, yes, darling. Do you have any better ideas? Because right now, I'm all ears. All was fine until he decided to stick that sodding railway line right through it all.'

I scoff. Talk about shitting on your own doorstep. I shake my head. 'It's all over then, Erin. Why are you doing this to me? You've got nowhere to put me.'

'We know it's all over. We're old and we're tired and we've come to terms with that. Which is exactly why we've chosen you. One last plaything and a fitting punishment for that man you were foolish enough to marry.'

My mind is racing. I can't focus on one thought for long enough to make sense of it all. Then, Oliver enters my mind. My gorgeous, sweet cat. An innocent party in this horror show.

'But, why did you kill my cat?' I ask her.

'Oh, we didn't do that. You must have more than one enemy. Hardly surprising, really.'

So that *was* Nana. As the thought of Nana enters my head, I see her poke her head up to peer through the window. She spies me tied up on the sofa, but her face remains expressionless. She dips down again and disappears. I tear my eyes away from the window, praying I didn't draw Erin's attention. Thankfully, it's fixed on her phone.

'Don't mind me, just texting Susan.'

Susan? It dawns on me like a punch to the stomach.

"S".

'Who's Susan?' I demand.

'Your other half's bit on the side,' she shrugs, still tapping away on the screen. 'She's a beautiful thing, too. Massive breasts, legs to die for. But, she's costing us an arm and a leg, so it'll be nice to relieve her from her duties.'

'You're paying her to sleep with Peter?!'

She nods. 'Yes. We needed her to feed us with information regarding the rail link project and given how promiscuous your husband is, the easiest way to do that was through pillow talk. She's been very useful. With her help, we have delayed the project by months. Buying us time.' She beams at me, and I feel sick. 'Time to get our affairs in order before playtime begins.'

CHAPTER THIRTY-TWO

'Greg, hi!' Erin says into the mouthpiece on her phone. She nods along to whatever her husband is saying. 'I've messaged Susan. She's keeping Peter occupied tonight, so all we can do is sit tight until Elijah is found, and then we can move her out.' She pauses. 'I know, honey. I love you, too.'

She says *love you* multiple times in decreasing volume before she hangs up the phone and turns to me. 'That was Greg,' she tells me unnecessarily. She flashes her teeth at me and places her phone on the coffee table that was shunted across the room in our scuffle. 'He's helping them find Elijah. He's such a good guy,' she says softly. 'Plus, the sooner the kid's found, the sooner we can get out of this dump.' She walks over to the window again and stares out wistfully. 'We've lived here our entire lives. We've had our difficulties, especially with that bitch Laura, but on the whole it's been good.'

'What happened with Laura?' My eyes are straining to see through the net curtains. Is Nana still there? Has she gone to get help, or has she just gone back inside to watch porn? I have to keep Erin talking.

'Laura made claims that weren't true. Tried to blackmail us with some nonsense that Elijah is Greg's. Nonsense. Greg wouldn't touch her with a barge pole; she's too stiff, too boring.'

'Greg slept with Laura?'

'She had the nerve to claim Greg took her without consent, but that's not his style, you know? If he wanted her like that, he'd let me join in. It's how we work.'

Bile rises in my throat. I only know a fraction of the story, but given that Erin has tied me up in my own living room, I have no doubt that Laura is telling the truth.

I wriggle my wrists furiously. The knots are loosening, I'm sure of it. If I angle my cast, I can dig it underneath the rope and if I'm patient, I know I can work the rope loose. I just wish every movement didn't feel like someone searing my arm with a red-hot poker.

'Was it you who broke into my house?' I ask, eager to distract her attention away from my back.

Erin laughs. 'You can blame Greg for that one, he's a prankster at heart. Plus, he wanted to wind Nana up. Silly old bat.'

I pause and look at Erin. 'I thought you cared for her?'

'Oh, please. That crazy cow needed shipping off to the loony bin years ago.'

'Then why? Why offer to help her?'

'She was fun to play with,' Erin shrugs. 'Besides, they say to keep your enemies close. When Laura went to Nana about Greg's "rape", Nana believed her and tried to persuade Laura to go to the police. Thank God, Laura knew she was full of lies and never bothered.'

None of this makes sense. How did helping Nana keep their secrets?

She continues. 'It turns out that doubling the dose of Nana's medication sends her over the edge of sanity. So, nobody would believe her. We just had to keep on top of it. Easy, really.'

'*You* did this to her? You made her this way?'

'Yes and no. She was a lunatic, anyway. We just made it more obvious.'

Poor Nana. Poor Kay. Erin and Greg are clearly unhinged, and now they have me tied up in my living room. This doesn't bode well for me.

Erin turns to look into the mirror above the fireplace. She runs her fingers through her hair and dabs lipstick from the corner of her mouth.

'You're sick,' I spit.

She turns to me, her face a picture of fury. 'Sick? No, darling, there's nothing sick about loving your husband so much you'd kill for them. I have no doubt you would have agreed with me a couple of months ago. You know what it's like to lose a baby. Now imagine *never* being able to provide that for the one you love. It makes you see things differently ...'

'Don't you dare talk about my baby!' My broken arm finally pops out of my restraints and before I have a chance to second-guess myself, I swing it at her. My bound ankles trip me up and my entire body weight smashes into her.

She stumbles back into the fireplace and her head hits the mantle with an excruciating crack. I reflexively reach out to her, but recoil when I see her eyes roll into the back of her head. She hits the floor with a heavy thump, shaking the mantle. I hover over her, watching. My ears ring with shock.

So, when her eyes suddenly fly open, it makes me jump and I grab the nearest thing to me. I slam the stone Buddah down hard, smashing it into her skull. The crack is agonisingly loud. Her mouth bobs open, but all that comes out is a wet gurgle before she loses consciousness. I stand over her, my hand clamped on my mouth. Blood is pooling around her head on the carpet, reaching for my feet. The Buddah is lying on my blood-stained pretty pink rug, smiling up at me. A picture of bliss.

I gulp and try to pull myself together. What do I do now? I need to get help. I sit on the floor and pull off the rope wrapped around my ankles. Then, I force my body up, and I hear him before I see him.

'What the fuck have you done to my wife?'

Chapter Thirty-Three

I turn to face Greg.

A sound escapes me, somewhere between a squeak and a cry. Greg's face is the deepest shade of crimson, but he doesn't look at me. He charges straight for his wife and kneels by her side, dropping the knife he was clutching by his side. I stare at its curve and decorative handle, willing myself to grab it, but fear and guilt overwhelm me and tears prickle my eyes.

I can't move. I can't save myself. I'm such a fool. Here is a man who enjoys torturing women. He's here for me, and yet I stand still. He's leaning over his possibly dead wife and yet here I am, waiting to be punished. What is wrong with me?

He strokes his wife's hair and dabs at the gash on the back of her head. Greg may be evil, but he sure knows how to love. 'It's time to go,' he eventually croaks. I just stare at him, my mouth bobbing open and closed.

He stands with incredible speed, making me jump back. 'Get the fuck out of here, now!' he screams in my face. I can smell the coffee on his breath. Coffee and fury. He's radiating heat, and I can see every pore on his puce face. I want to take a step back, but I'm blocked by the sofa.

He yells and grabs my hair, yanking my head down to his waist. He pulls me towards the door, and I stumble after him. My knees hit the floor, but he keeps dragging me. Pain rips through my skull as I scramble to catch up with him to ease the sting in my scalp.

The street is quiet now, darkness has set in, and people have either given up the search for Elijah in favour of their dinner, or Elijah has been found. I hope it's the latter.

Now that I'm out of the house, I feel bolder and try to scream, but the second I open my mouth, Greg rams my face into my car as we pass it, denting the door panel and sending shockwaves of pain down my face and neck. Instead, I whimper quietly, like a good girl. Rain cascades down, feeding the chaos.

'Now, sit there and be good,' he tells me, as he pushes me into the passenger seat of his battered brown van. He buckles my seatbelt like I am a child.

When he takes his seat beside me, my memories throw me back to the night I arrived here with Peter. I remember looking at him, the love of my life, driving along, happiness oozing out of us. It was supposed to be the start of something so special, so magical. I had dreams back then. Nothing extravagant. I have never asked for much.

Love. That's what I wanted. Simple love. The kind that makes you feel comfortable and secure. The type of love that ebbs and flows – the undercurrent constant, but when you stand still, it overwhelms you.

I haven't even got an ounce of that. Soon, I might not even have my life. I will die not having experienced true love. I press my face to the glass window as tears pour from my eyes, blurring the countryside that rolls past.

'Sorry you lost your baby,' Greg mumbles, his words interrupted by the swish of his wipers. 'I didn't know you were pregnant.'

As if this man has an ounce of compassion to care enough about a dead foetus. How dare he speak of my baby!

'I didn't expect you to be in the car.'

I slowly turn to face him, realising what Greg is saying, kicking me in the gut.

'We thought if we put Peter out of action for a while, it'd buy us time with the railway project. But, it turns out, it did nothing at all.'

'*You* tampered with the car?'

He doesn't say anything.

'*You* killed my baby?!' I ram my shoulder into him, making him jerk the steering wheel to the right. Trees plough towards us, but he regains control before we make impact. He catches my eye just before he raises his fist.

Then blackness descends.

It could be minutes or it could be hours later when I regain consciousness. Greg is pulling off the country road and heading down a narrow track. Branches reach out and claw at the side of the van, the scraping unbearably loud in my pounding head.

'You hurt my Erin,' Greg says, his voice crackly. 'You hurt her.' He sounds incredulous. I expect he's not used to his victims fighting back. That fills me with an immense sense of dread.

'I didn't mean to kill her,' I squeak. I pray she's not dead - I'm not a killer. Am I?

'No!' he roars. 'You deliberately killed my wife! Whereas I never meant for you to be in that car!' He yanks the door open and pushes his way out into the rain, slamming the door behind him, making the van rock.

I brace myself, my whimpers loud. He reaches my side and pulls my door open, pulling me out by my broken arm. Something shifts inside the cast, and I swear I feel my bone break again. I scream.

But, there's no one here to hear me. I am surrounded by nothing but trees and darkness. There are no car sounds, no headlights flashing through the tree trunks. There is absolutely no sign of life. Given the number of victims Greg has taken over the years without being caught, there is no way anyone is going to find me.

A small cottage appears in front of us. It's dilapidated, but I imagine in different circumstances I could see the potential. By the way the stone is crumbling around the wonky front door, and the lack of roof in places, I guess this house has not been lived in for decades.

Except for Greg's victims.

I stumble and look down at my feet, expecting to see a tree root. There isn't a root, just a strange, long mound of earth.

A grave.

We approach the house and Greg unlocks a hefty bolt attached to the door instead of a door handle. The door pushes open with a groan, and he pushes me into the darkness. I fall to the floor, scraping my elbows on filth-infested stone.

Greg wanders off and I can hear him through the darkness, pulling out drawers with a clatter. My eyes roam around the room, desperately trying to find clues as to where I am and how I can escape, but without light I can only just make out the beams on the ceiling.

The smell is overwhelming. The unmistakable metallic tang of blood makes me gag and I have to force myself to control my breathing to keep from throwing up. There is also the unmistakable stench of urine coming from the rear of the room.

Greg lights a candle, the glow throwing a surprising amount of light over the space. I fall back. My eyes whirl around the room, but there is just too much to take in and I feel dizzy.

Tools are hung neatly along the wall to my left. Some are small: pliers, hammers, and chisels. Some are larger: saws, an axe, a crowbar. There is a rack dedicated to knives – some plain kitchen knives, some of a more elaborate design, others that look like mini saws.

In the room is a hospital trolley, complete with stirrups. A weird leather block sits in the centre of the room. The corners contain stacks of rags, presumably for cleaning.

Sobs pour out of me in thick, noisy wails. This can't be happening to me. Things like this happen in movies and books, not real life.

'Oh, shut up. You deserve everything you get,' Greg says, horrifyingly calm. He's lighting more candles and placing them around the room. 'Candles,' he says. 'Adds a touch of romance, don't you think?'

I don't say anything, and he shrugs at me.

When he finishes, he returns to the bench that contained the candles and places his hands on the surface. With his eyes raised to the ceiling, he says, 'This is for you, Erin.' Tremors course through me.

He turns to me with a smile. 'Did Erin tell you you're my last?' He waits for me to reply, but gives up when it's obvious I'm incapable of speaking. He continues. 'Thanks to that fella of yours, our extracurricular activities are done for.' He looks into my eyes, his stare tearing me open. I feel like my soul is exposed for this monster to devour. 'So, *Jen*,' he purrs my name. 'I think we should have some fun. What do you think?'

'You're sick,' I spit back.

He laughs, but the sound doesn't match his voice. It's high-pitched and cackly, like a witch. 'Oh, my darling, you think I don't know that already? The thing is …' He turns to the wall containing the rows of knives and runs an index finger over them. 'I just don't care.'

He pauses at a gap in his disgusting display and scratches his head. The pause unnerves me; what is he cooking up for me?

Eventually, he shrugs and steps over to me, where I'm nervously looking at the only way out. I go to open my mouth, but he slaps me so hard I fall down. He looks down at me, willing me to cry, but I won't give him the satisfaction. He squats so that we're face to face. He gently tilts my chin upwards, and our lips brush together.

I twist away with a grunt, but he's too quick and squeezes my cheeks together, bunching my mouth into a pout. 'Don't be silly, now. The more you fight, the more exciting it is for me. And the more excited I get …' He grins and runs a finger over my breast, mimicking what Erin did to me in my house. 'The more carried away I get. You want to see my last girl, Jen? She was lovely.'

'No,' I whisper.

'What did you say?' He asks me, but he's already walking away and collecting a shoe box off the bench. By the time he gets back to me, he's pulled out a polaroid picture.

'Look at this beauty. Erin thought she looked like Elsa from *Frozen*.' He hesitates showing me the photo, his anguish over Erin making him falter.

I wish he'd faltered for longer. The photo is of a girl, her limbs long and strong and her skin pure white and smooth. She looks young. Far too young. But then, is there an age deserving of *this*?

She's bound with rope and tied to the strange leather box in the middle of the room. She's bent over it, her body mutilated with hundreds of bruises and cuts. The photo is taken from her rear, leaving nothing to the imagination. She's open wide where Greg has inserted tools into her two openings.

I can't see her face, but the way her head droops forward, her hair flopping to the side, tells me she's dead. By the state of her body, I hope she is.

'No!' The word heaves out of me as a scream. I'm screaming for this poor girl. I'm screaming for me. I'm screaming that people this sick and twisted walk freely amongst us. For all the pain Peter has put me through, it is nothing compared to this. I didn't know this level of evil could exist.

Greg drags over a chain from the wall and amidst my screams, begins to tie me up.

'No!' I continue to scream, though the word has lost all meaning. I try to yank away from him. I kick my legs out in every direction. I will fight. Greg will *not* do this to me.

Greg's fist lands on my eye socket, turning the world white. My body freezes. 'Now, now, Jen. I think we need to establish some rules. This is my place, and you should at least show me some respect in it.' He pushes my face into the floor.

I still can't see properly. My left eye is already starting to swell, blurring my vision. Dirt from the floor sucks into my mouth and nose. I can feel it enter my lungs.

'Let's begin,' Greg whispers into my ear, pushing me onto my front. He yanks my jeans down to my knees and wolfwhistles. 'You've got a perfect ass, dear.' He bites it. Hard. I feel blood trickle down over my hip.

I'm sobbing, powerless to do anything.

He spreads my cheeks and I grit my teeth and wait. *If I'm a good girl, he'll be gentle*. I tell myself.

If I'm a good girl, he'll be gentle.

I grit my teeth.

But, he takes too long. Nothing happens. I can hear him breathing, then his breaths turn into gasps. His gasps turn into a wheeze and then his body weight smashes into me.

Then, stillness. Greg doesn't move.

He's lying on me awkwardly and I realise I can't hear his deep, gruff breaths anymore. Something warm is dripping over my back and legs. I try to shuffle away, but he's too heavy and my movements are restricted by the chains.

'I've got this, sweetie.' Her voice drifts over as if from the heavens.

Greg slides off me in small, jerky movements, and I sit up. He's lying on the floor, a butcher's knife dug into his neck. The handle is curved and intricate.

Nana leans over him, smiling like she's just won a round of bingo.

CHAPTER THIRTY-FOUR

I pull up my blood-covered jeans, my fingers sliding over the slick button. Nana, completely unphased by the events, starts wittering on about how her husband once dreamt of owning a cabin in the woods while I stagger around, searching for Greg's phone.

I rifle through the bench, retching at the hundreds of images of girls. Most are tied to Greg's play-apparatus in a myriad of positions and with a variety of wounds. Some photos show girls alive, or at least somewhere between life and death. Other girls are clearly dead and yet still subject to Greg's version of "play".

Erin has clearly been the keen photographer, but occasionally there are photos of her dressing the girls in outfits like they're oversized dolls. By the crease of her brow, I can tell she's clearly not eager to touch them. I imagine Greg forcing her to go against her will. I'd sympathise, but then I remember she is just as sick as he is. She can rot in hell, too.

I find his phone on a small shelf by the door and drag Nana outside while calling the police. The rear door of Greg's van is wide open, and Nana's presence suddenly makes sense. If Greg had checked his van before driving off, this situation would have played out completely differently. I suspect Nana would be dead, and I would be living in hell right now.

The rain has stopped, but the wind is howling so I stand next to the van in the hope it offers some form of shelter. My entire body aches. My arm is in agony. The bite mark on my backside throbs. I want to cry, but I can't; now is not the time to lose control. I just need to stay calm until help arrives. A lump forms in my throat, a mockery to my resolve.

'The police are coming, Nana,' I tell her, still on the phone to emergency services. Sweat is dripping down my spine, but I shiver violently. The woman on the phone is saying something, but I'm too busy searching for Nana to register her words. 'Nana?'

A cloud shifts and moonlight suddenly pours through the tree branches. I see her resting under a tree, the light providing a perfect spotlight, a perfect halo. I smile. She looks so happy, so peaceful. What an amazing woman.

'Nana!' I tread my way over to her and kneel down to hold her hand. She turns to smile at me, and she looks spent.

She's my hero.

'Police are a couple of minutes away. You'll hear their sirens any second,' the operator tells me and sure enough, sirens drift across the woods. They're coming from my right, so I imagine that's where the main road must lie.

I stroke Nana's hand. It's cold. 'Nana, you should wake up,' I whisper. But, something is off. I peer closer and rest my hand on her heart.

I speak into the phone. 'Can you call an ambulance, too? My friend ... She's dead.'

CHAPTER THIRTY-FIVE

From my room, I watch him arrive. He walks over to the receptionist looking sheepish, but as soon as he is approached by the pretty nurse, a smile sweeps across his face and he turns on his charismatic charm. He sickens me. When he sees me watching him, he switches his face to look more mournful. Apparently suave is not a good look for someone who's supposed to be melancholy. I turn away, unable to make eye contact with him.

'Jen-Jen?' he says as he approaches my bed, jerking me out of my contemplations.

'Yes?' I slowly look up at him, determined not to show him a hint of emotion. I have come through far too much to let this piece of shit bother me.

'Are you okay?'

I laugh. Okay, that was funny. 'What do you think, Peter? Kidnapped, almost raped, smashed Erin around the head, and to top things off, I watched Nana die. Now let me think ... Am I okay?' I tap my finger on my chin.

'You don't need to be facetious.'

'And you don't need to be a compulsive liar, yet here we are.'

'Is that why you did it? Because I was cheating on you?'

The arsehole has already switched topics. His level of selfishness will never cease to shock me. I feign confusion, despite knowing exactly what he's talking about. I want to make him sweat. 'I have no idea what you're talking about.'

'Oh, don't give me that. The police have already been round, asking me all kinds of questions. They seem to think I've been abusing you. They talked about *rape*, for Christ's sake.'

He's turning a deeper shade of red, and I force myself not to smile. I am well aware that I will never be able to prove what Peter has done to me. The police have probably already reached a dead end. But, if I can at the very least scare that arrogance out of him, then I've won something. I'll be watching him like a hawk from now on. No girl is going to go through what I did.

He doesn't scare me anymore. And there's not a drop of love left.

'You can't do this to me, Jen. I hold my hands up. I shouldn't have cheated on you, but you can't punish me by lying to the police. It's disgusting. I've lost all respect for you.'

I can't hold back anymore and laughter bursts out of me so hard, spit sprinkles over his face. He steps back, repulsed by me. Good. 'What's funny?' he barks.

'You think I care about your mistress? And Peter, the only person lying here is *you*. You're lying to yourself if you believe you're fucking innocent in all this.' I sit up in my bed and jab a finger at him. 'You are a sick piece of scum who is so delusional you have absolutely *no* idea who you are and what you're capable of. People like you end up dying alone. Karma is a bitch, Peter, and you'll get exactly what you deserve.' I pause to catch my breath. 'Oh, and your mistress was a hooker, Peter.

She was *paid* to sleep with you. I hope she was paid a lot, too – the poor cow deserves a fortune.'

He sneers. 'Bollocks. Jealousy is not a good look on you, Jen.'

'Jealous,' I tease the word around my mouth, unsure what to do with it. 'Peter, I suggest you leave here and run. Kay has spread the news about your involvement with the railway line. The people in Thistlewood are not going to be pleased with you.'

'Well, they needn't bother.' He looks at me with pure poison. 'The project has been cancelled. Forensics are all over the place and the government has decided it wouldn't look good to be sticking a railway track over a burial site.'

'Oh, what a shame,' I tell him, sarcasm dripping from my voice.

He takes another step back. 'I have no idea who you are anymore, Jen. You used to be so sweet, so good.'

'Yeah? That's funny, because now I know exactly who I am.'

CHAPTER THIRTY-SIX

I push my sunglasses from my head onto my nose. The heat from the sun coats me in comfort and I sigh into the breeze, releasing the tension in my shoulders.

I'm shocked by how many people are here. At least one hundred people are lurking around, some restraining their delight at seeing long-forgotten friends, some saddened by the sombre occasion, some lost amongst the confusion of how to behave.

This is only the second funeral I have attended. Mum thought I was too young to attend my father's funeral and then the next one was hers, and it was a nasty affair. The rain attacked her grave, showing no mercy, and the few friends who did attend left after the ceremony, leaving me alone with a buffet and an emptiness I didn't know how to handle.

Today is different. Today, we are here to celebrate.

Listening in on conversations, I've learnt that Nana touched many lives in her years as a teacher. She was someone who went out of her way to inject a dose of optimism into people. She wanted to help people beyond their academics and people have been coming forward all day, desperate to give their thanks.

'I remember when she rescued the puppy from my nasty next-door neighbour. I told so many people that the dog was being abused, but only Mrs Gardner was willing to stand up and do something about it,' said one mourner.

'Mrs Gardner once brought round a hamper on Christmas Eve. If it wasn't for her, we would have had a frozen lasagne for Christmas dinner,' said another.

'Nana listened to me when I was sixteen and pregnant,' said someone through tears. 'I had no one else to turn to. If it wasn't for her, I have no doubt I wouldn't have my incredible son today. He's a firefighter now!'

I hide in the corner, ashamed to have been part of Nana's death. Guilt eats at me and I'm wondering when it would be an acceptable time to leave, when Kay comes over.

'Thanks for coming,' she says. I have seen her a couple of times since everything happened. Now that I'm no longer living next door, she isn't as approachable, and I didn't want to go around there and interrupt the grief of the poor woman and her children.

I did see her at the hospital, though. She popped her head around my curtain and asked if I was okay. I tried to explain to her, but she held up her hand to stop me, shook her head, and walked away. The next time I saw her was in the police station. Her face was streaked with tears. She didn't see me, and I hung back to give her space. Now, she stands before me looking radiant. Her smile is sad, but beautiful. I'm torn between wanting to run and wanting to embrace her.

'It's no bother, Kay. I didn't know whether I should be here.'

'Why not?' She looks genuinely shocked.

I swallow. 'Because if it wasn't for me ...'

She places a hand on my shoulder. 'You can stop that right now.' She dips her head to look deeper into my eyes. 'This isn't your fault. Nana died saving you. That was *her* choice, and it was honestly the best way for her to go.'

'But, she would still be here if ...'

'Maybe. But, she made that choice and I've come to realise she would have been satisfied with it, and I have to feel the same. Plus, Jen, her heart gave out. That might have happened when she was playing snakes and ladders with the girls. *That* wasn't the right way for her. Nana died *when* she was saving you, not *because* she was saving you.'

I feel my head tip back. My shoulders droop and my chest feels bigger, and for the first time in months I can finally breathe. Kay pulls me in for a hug and I hold her as much as she holds me. We're united. With all the evil in the world, nothing can dampen the light of the good.

The room suddenly quietens, and Kay lets go of me. We turn to face where everyone's attention is drawn and see Laura walking towards us. There are bags under her eyes that rival my own. Her hair is pulled into a loose ponytail and her dress is loose over her thinning frame. I have never seen her without makeup before and I'm surprised to see she suffers terrible acne scarring.

She walks slowly, as if through quicksand. When she's standing before us there's an awkward silence.

'I just came to say I'm sorry,' she tells Kay.

Kay just nods. I don't know whether I should stay or go and leave them to their conversation. I opt to stay so as not to draw attention to myself. The day after Elijah went missing and was subsequently found with his fingers wrapped around the neck of the pub owner's cat, Chinese whispers erupted through the community. I didn't know what the truth was, so I ignored them all and waited for the truth.

I feel the wait is over.

'What are you apologising for?' Kay asks her.

'Please don't do this.'

'No, I need to hear it from you. What are you apologising for?'

Laura shuffles and glances around the room. Most people are watching her, but she doesn't shy away. 'Elijah,' she whispers. 'He's a troubled boy. But, I swear to you, I only just found out. If I'd known sooner ...'

'What has he done, Laura?'

'He was the one who set fire to the school.'

Kay nods. 'The fire everyone blamed Nana for?'

Laura nods.

'Anything else?'

'He smashed the windows in the shop, too.'

'And?'

'And for breaking into those houses.'

Kay nods. 'You know he destroyed Nana's reputation. Do you know how miserable she's been these last couple of years? She was an incredibly clever, kind woman, diminished to being a crazy woman with violent tendencies.'

'I'm sorry.'

Kay breathes in deeply. 'If it were me, I'd pound one in your face right now. But, this is about Nana. She wouldn't want that.' She looks carefully at Laura, her head cocked to the side. 'Is Elijah getting help?'

Laura sobs. 'Yes, they took him away from me.'

I bring my hand to my mouth.

'But, they'll help him,' Kay tries to convince her. 'And you're there for him. You and Harry.'

For the first time, Laura glances at me. 'Yes, me and Harry,' she says with conviction. So, she's still with him. Given her desperate circumstances, I'm not surprised.

She turns to speak to me. 'I wanted to say sorry to you, too.' Tears drip over her cheeks.

'For what?' I can't think of anything she might have done to me.

'Your cat.'

That's all she has to say. Elijah killed Oliver. The earth moves under my feet and my hands clench into fists by my side. I feel Kay's bare arm press against mine and I release my grip. I will learn from Kay, this woman of honour, and remain calm.

'I never wanted him to turn out this way. I always thought nurture beat nature, but now I know that's just not true.'

Kay makes a noise, signifying her confusion, but I know exactly what Laura is blabbering on about. Elijah is Greg's son.

I try to reach out to her, but she shrugs me off and turns to leave. Kay stops her and speaks for the both of us. 'Laura? I think we just need some space right now. But, I do hope that one day we can support each other.'

Laura smiles weakly. She's broken. She's a victim in all this, too. She's locked away in her massive house desperately trying to cling on to the threads of her life. The more she's pulled, the more her life has frayed. I don't know what has happened with Elijah, but I bet this is killing her more than it can ever hurt us.

'I would like that, too,' I say. 'I could use a friend.'

Kay gives my hand a squeeze and Laura looks at each of us in turn. She nods and her facial features soften. She exits the room.

EPILOGUE

'Squish, come here!' I still cringe at the name, but the impact is starting to lessen with time. I tried to change her name. I had a bucket full of treats to aid training, but no matter what I did, "Squish" stuck.

My gorgeous boxer-lab mix has been in my life for a year. She's as headstrong and brave as I long to be and every day I learn from her. She comes from a background of abuse. As do I. She was alone. As was I. She was starved, and I was starved of love. We're united by our pasts, but together we can throw all that away and move forward. Admittedly, Squish is better at it than me, but I'm getting there.

She runs at me looking particularly pleased with the stick she has lodged in her mouth. It's so big that she whacks a man in the knee as she makes her way over to me. I wave an apology, but he just laughs. Squish has that effect on people – she spreads joy. How anyone could treat her badly is beyond me.

She arrives at my feet and drops her stick as a gift. 'Thanks, babe,' I tell her, patting her head. She sits still, waiting patiently for me to put her lead back on, her breath warm and damp in my face. 'Come on, girl, let's go.' It has been an absolutely beautiful day. The sun is still pouring out heat and it's gone seven o'clock.

My day at work could not have gone better. I have passed five of my chartered accountancy exams and the accountancy practice I work for sent me out alone to meet a client for the first time. I'm glowing from the confidence my manager has in me and I relish having my own project to work on from scratch. Plus, the client just so happened to be a baker, so my tummy is full of croissants and tarts.

I walk away from my apartment that sits above the corner shop. The same shop that was once victim to Elijah's curiosity for violence. As much as I had to leave Peter's house, I knew I couldn't leave Thistle-wood. I knew there was good here and now the chaff is gone, only a purity remains.

Peter soon moved on to pastures new and I took delight in seeing the house get snapped up by a young family who have injected life into the building. Chalk drawings litter the path outside, a campervan is parked in the drive, and when I paid Kay a visit, I heard laughter emanate through the walls.

The house deserves the happiness we couldn't give it.

Despite the bulk of the village gossip still centering around Greg and Erin, Gill still likes to pop up in people's conversations every now and then.

After I confronted her about her tax evasion, she seemed to just vanish into thin air and with the shock of Greg's torture chamber no one was particularly bothered. I haven't told anyone the police questioned me about her.

It turns out Gill is a prolific liar. For a start, her real name is Faith (the irony isn't lost on me). She has adopted many identities over the last thirty years and stolen hundreds of thousands of pounds through a multitude of scams.

Where that money is now, no one knows.

I know Faith graffitied my house. Only in hindsight could I marry up the handwriting on my house with that on her paperwork. Good luck to her. I know people always get what they deserve, eventually.

I continue strolling along with my face in my phone. I'm flicking through Laura's photos on Facebook. She's away this week, spending time with Elijah.

A lack of evidence meant Elijah was never punished for his actions, so I was stunned when Laura refused to let him live at home and packed him off to a notoriously strict boarding school.

'I just can't have him living at home,' Laura confessed over a glass of wine to me and Kay one evening. 'I don't think I know how to handle him, and without intervention I'm scared of the man he'll become.'

We nodded along but didn't say anything. It isn't our place to offer advice. Laura needs to arrive at this decision on her own and it sounds like a good plan.

In the year since Elijah left Thistlewood, he's transformed. He's studious, athletic, and popular. All the things a mother hopes for in their child. His school regularly reports on him and despite a few hiccups in the beginning, he's really screwed his head on.

The icing on the cake was when he wrote me a letter of apology for what he did to Oliver. I'm not naïve enough to think he's changed completely. When you've got bad in your heart, it'll live there forever, but I sure hope he can push it down.

'Squish!' I call out. I got too lost in the images of Laura grinning with her boy and have loosened my grip on her lead. She breaks away from me and runs across the road, narrowly dodging a speeding car who unhelpfully blares his horn at me. I take flight after her, my chest tight. She charges towards the duck pond and jumps in, super happy to be rolling amongst the reeds and making the ducks flap away. She turns to look at me, delighted that she's brought us to the green I have been trying to avoid.

Greg and Erin's house is still taped up. No one has bothered to take it down since their *hobbies* were discovered. Greg was swiftly buried without ceremony and after a grilling from the police, Erin was imprisoned in a high-security unit a hundred miles away from here. She confessed to everything and not a single body has been unaccounted for. The bitch lived.

Forty-two.

Forty-two young women subject to torture and murder at the hands of that couple. When I think too closely that I broke that chain, it devastates me. Why should I be the lucky one? Why not one of the forty-two girls that came before me?

I know I am yet to examine my emotions surrounding everything that has happened here, and when I do, it's going to hurt. For now, I'm sitting tight and letting my wounds heal in the hope I'll be stronger and more capable when the PTSD takes hold.

I grab Squish by the collar and yank her out of the water. I would be angry, but her grin has the power to wipe away all irritation and replace it with laughter.

We walk together now, and I avoid looking at the abandoned thatched cottage I used to love so much. I can only focus on my future, and that house is firmly placed in my past.

The pub is bustling as people take advantage of the Friday evening sun. A few people call out to me as I enter.

'Here she is!' Kay calls over, waving us to a table in the corner. She's already bought me a glass of wine and it sits invitingly, condensation dripping down the side. We greet each other warmly, though much of Kay's affection is directed at Squish, who revels in her affection.

Kay catches me up on her date last night. Unlike me, Kay is ready to meet someone, but she's being super picky and hearing her antics brings me out in fits of giggles.

'He was wearing a fedora, Jen. A fedora!'

'Oh, jeez. Didn't he get the no-hat memo?'

'Exactly!'

My phone buzzes in my pocket. 'Sara,' I tell Kay, answering the call. I wouldn't say I'm Sara's best friend, but there's a respect between us that sits comfortably in my life. When I left Peter, she called me to apologise. She knew Peter was bad, but she thought it was solely directed at her. Sara thought *she* was to blame. It never crossed her mind that it was Peter who brought the trouble, and then brought that same trouble to me. I forgave her. I can't place blame on another victim.

'Hi!' I chirp. It's unusual for Sara to call out of the blue. 'You okay?'

'Jen, have you heard?' Her voice is weirdly dark.

'Heard what?'

'It's Peter. He's dead.'

I smile. Karma really is a bitch.

LIKE WHAT YOU READ?

There's more!

For free books, competitions, news on the author and general silliness, sign up to the mailing list at subscribepage.io/ejJ56y

Or join in the fun on Facebook by searching for '**C.L. Sutton Author**'

Alternatively, drop me an email at **hello@clsutton.com** and I will endeavour to reply to you personally.

Thank you from the bottom of my heart

It means so much to me that you have taken the time to read my book. A monumental amount of time, effort, and love is poured into every book written and I think I speak for all authors when I say we are grateful for your support.

If you want to help give my book a boost, please consider leaving a review and recommending me to your friends. It's a HUGE help.

OTHER BOOKS BY C.L. SUTTON

H ave you read *Killing for Innocence*?

How far would you go to protect the innocent?

Michelle's life is on the brink of collapse, and she has never truly got over the abuse she experienced at the hands of her parents. Now, living in her friend's spare bedroom and relying on alcohol for comfort, she's not sure she'll ever end the spiral of self-destruction.

When successful and glamorous Pam recruits Michelle to work at her charity helping victims of child abuse, Michelle finally finds her calling.

But when Pam's requests take a dark turn, an inner darkness awakens in Michelle, throwing her into a world of secrets, pain, and murder. A life more exciting than Michelle dare admit.

It's only when seven-year-old Teddy, a child close to her heart, goes miss-ing, does Michelle realise her quest is so much bigger than she imagined. And so much more brutal.

Killing for Innocence *is a spectacular standalone psychological thriller by C.L. Sutton that features dark themes, raw emotions, and superb plot twists.*

Acknowledgements

I did it! Again!

One book is one thing but to put myself through it again is something else. It's a labour of love and I love every bit of it, especially the hair pulling part.

Once again I need to thank my husband. My supporter. My encouragement. V, you have no idea what it means to have your support. I am realising my childhood dreams and not once have you laughed or scoffed. I love you.

My friends and editors Ali and Erin. Your expertise is forever appreciated, and I am in awe of your kindness and generosity of time. You're so special to me and I hope you know that.

Finally, thank you to YOU, my reader. For giving me a chance and following Jen-Jen on her journey.

Made in the USA
Coppell, TX
24 May 2024

32727507R00132